*A*
*Harlequin*
*Romance*

# THE FEATHERED SHAFT

*by*

### JANE ARBOR

———————————————

**HARLEQUIN**     **BOOKS**

**Winnipeg • Canada**     **New York • New York**

———————————————

THE FEATHERED SHAFT

First published in 1970 by Mills & Boon Limited,
17 - 19 Foley Street, London, England.

Harlequin Canadian edition published November, 1970
Harlequin U.S. edition published February, 1971

Standard Book Number: 373-51443-3.

Printed in Canada

# CHAPTER ONE

THAT afternoon the warm spring sunshine after a week of rain had brought people out in their thousands to shop, to stroll, to sightsee and to crowd the café terraces in search of tea and ices and gossip with friends.

In consequence, an empty table on the open-air balcony of the Hotel Vaucluse was a prize at which Nicola had snatched as soon as it was vacated by a girl whose departure was as hurried as was her own pounce on the table, forestalling a stout matron by a triumphant metre or so.

Nicola had relaxed blissfully in the comfortable cane chair. From now on for about three weeks—longer perhaps, if the money spun out!—there was no need to hurry. Her days were her own to spend as she pleased. And she knew she intended to 'please' by enjoying Lausanne, its enchanting Lac Léman and its breathtaking backdrop of mountain, to the full. Because for this—or for anywhere similar where the chances of her job had taken her this spring—she had kept assignments in London and Leeds and Bristol, and once in an ice-bound Glasgow, throughout the long winter, promising herself that she would go hot-foot after the very first Continental posting that offered.

So that when, a month ago, the agency for which she worked freelance had rung up—'Are you free,

Miss Stirling? We have a trade delegation—Balliol Bros., English cut glass—needing a bi-lingual secretary and interpreter for the period of a month's sales conference in Lausanne,' she had said only, 'Yes, I'm free. Give me details, will you?'—and a few hours later had been on her way.

It had been a hectic four weeks. But now the salesman minions of 'Balliol Bros.' had taken themselves back to England, well pleased with the business they had done, and Nicola was left with a most satisfactory wad of currency in her bag. She had hired a small car and would use it now for a nostalgic tour of the region she had known five years ago—Vevey, Montreux, Evian across the Lake, the mountains ... Yes, she could afford to give herself this holiday, since for trained secretaries with two foreign languages at their tongues' end there were always good jobs to be had.

It was as well she was not impatient to be served with tea, for the waiter was a long time in scurrying her way. And when at last he did he was unhelpful in the matter of the small bunch of keys with an address tagged to one of them which Nicola had found on the table when she took it.

She offered them to him. 'The lady who was here before me must have left them,' she explained.

The boy looked blank. 'But she has gone, *mademoiselle*. I do not know her. I have no way of——'

Nicola cut in, 'There's an address on them. You should hand them in to the office to be called for.'

He fingered the bunch reluctantly. 'The office is three floors down, *mademoiselle*. And I am very busy, as you see——'

'You should still take them. Hand them in when you do have time. You can't leave them here. They are going to be missed quite soon.'

A tired sigh. 'As you say, *mademoiselle*——' But before the keys were dropped into his trouser pocket Nicola changed her mind. Convinced he would forget them, she held out her hand. 'That address—let me look. I think I have to pass it on my way home. If you like, I'll undertake to deliver them instead?'

Little as he should have trusted her, clearly he 'liked' enough to hand over the keys. 'A thousand thanks, *mademoiselle*. You are very kind!' Then he scribbled her tea-chit, anchored it under a plate and hurried away, to reappear no more.

Half an hour later Nicola collected her parked car. As she moved off it occurred to her that she might have handed in the keys herself. But the address—an apartment on an avenue she knew well—shouldn't be too hard to find. She only hoped the door of the flat had a letter-box, that was all.

The block was a modern service one with a lift, and as Nicola emerged on to the corridor of the first floor she saw the door of Number Nine being opened by a concierge, while the late occupant of Nicola's tea-table stood by.

The man withdrew his pass-key with a flourish. '*Et voilà, madame!*'

'Oh, thank you. For your trouble, *monsieur*——' The girl fumbled in her bag; a tip changed hands and Nicola quickened her pace.

'Excuse me, but I think these may be your keys. You left them——' she began, then halted to stare . . . surprised, puzzled, searching for a name as the girl turned, frowned and seemed to be in the same perplexity herself.

They found what they wanted in chorus.

'Diane—Thesige, isn't it?'

'Nicola—Nicola Stirling!'

They nodded, laughed, offered their hands and Diane touched Nicola's cheeks with her lips. Then they were babbling pleasurably.

'After all this time!'

'How long *is* it since Vevey?'

'What are you doing in Lausanne?'

'What are *you*? In an apartment? I thought your home was in Neuchâtel—wasn't it?' As a thought struck Nicola, 'You're not married, by any chance?'

'Married?' Diane's echo was sharp. 'No. No, nothing like that. Yes, Neuchâtel. We are still there, Kurt and I. Father died. It's Kurt I'm here with now—— But come in. We must talk. Kurt is out and he won't be back yet.'

In the typically characterless living-room of the furnished flat they chattered on, the coincidence of the lost keys which had led to their meeting forgotten as they filled in for each other the years since 'Vevey'— which they both made their shorthand phrase for the exclusive finishing-school where Diane had been a pupil and where Nicola, three years the senior, had taught English conversation for two years in exchange for the perfection of her Italian and French, with a view to the specialised secretarial work she had done ever since.

Diane, then seventeen, had had another year at Vevey after Nicola had gone back to England. 'Which makes you twenty-two now,' Nicola calculated aloud.

'And since then?'

'Since? Well, Neuchâtel—at home, that is.' As she talked Diane moved restlessly about the room. 'With our Aunt Agathe, who runs the house for Kurt. She is rather delicate and elderly—much older than Father, and he was nearly seventy when he died. He'd married very late, you see, and he was over forty when Kurt was born. Father died soon after you left Vevey. You never met Kurt, did you?'

'Your brother? No.'

'Yes, well—I'm afraid Father kept him out of *Thesige* for far too long—you know, our horology firm, clocks and watches and things?'

Nicola did indeed know *Thesige*. It was a name on railway platforms, on billboards on auto-routes; at night it flashed in neons above city streets, side by side with names like Menier and Cyma and Suchard and Bally—all household words far beyond Swiss borders. She nodded. 'Of course, I remember. But Kurt is in charge now?'

'Oh yes. And going ahead where Father refused to —into precision stuff for aircraft and ships and computers. He works all the hours there are. And that's why he's here now—on a kind of export drive. Conventions and entertaining overseas buyers and staging an exhibition in the Palais de Beaulieu. Lausanne is that kind of place, you know.'

Nicola confirmed, 'I do. I came myself as secretary to an English firm's sales mission. So you are going to be here while your brother is? How long will that be?'

'He doesn't know. Possibly several weeks. I came as a kind of a social hostess for him—helping to entertain the business wives while he looks after the men. My

English and Italian aren't bad, and I can just get by in German if I have to.'

'And in American too, I hope?' teased Nicola.

But Diane wasn't listening. After perching briefly on a chair-arm, she began to prowl again. She found cigarettes and offered them. Lighting her own and flicking imaginary ash from it, she went on, 'For the moment I'm having to be Kurt's chauffeur too. His only relaxation is squash rackets and he had sprained his wrist slightly the day before we left home to come here. That was yesterday. We——'

'Oh, only then?' put in Nicola. 'Then I shall be here for some of the time you are. I'm free now, and I meant to have a bit of a holiday. So perhaps we could see something of each other whenever you're free yourself? I'd like that, if you would.'

'Yes ... Yes. We shall have to arrange something ... some time.' But Diane's tone was laconic, and sensing a snub she had not expected, Nicola glanced at her quickly.

Saving them both embarrassment, Diane looked away, then back again for an adroit change of subject.

Studying Nicola, 'You know, you haven't changed a bit in—what is it, five years?' she said. 'Do you remember how we expected you to be our idea of "the English Mees"—all pudding-plump and pink-and-white? And you weren't a bit—with your dark eyes and those fabulous eyelashes that we had to envy because in those days we didn't dare experiment with falsies. And your *rather* wide mouth, and your high cheekbones—more like a Slav. And you don't look a day older than then.'

'Well, what do you expect in only five years?'

laughed Nicola. 'That I'd have grown crowsfeet and be hobbling on a stick? Have a heart! And come to that'—appraising Diane's own dark hair and finely etched features—'don't we all look much of an age nowadays until we're pushing forty or so—if then?'

'M'm. Perhaps.' Diane's agreement was again laconic, and her next question was quite out of context.

'Men, Nicola? What about them—for you?'

Nicola shrugged. 'Well, naturally, here and there. But nothing serious. And for you?'

Diane looked away again. 'Yes, there's been—one,' she admitted, then moved over to the window to run a fingernail over the slats of the Venetian blind, closed against the hot afternoon sun. Nicola waited. 'And is one still?' she prompted at last.

At that Diane turned. 'In a way—yes.' She looked at her watch. 'Kurt should be back soon. He had to see a man at the Belgian Consulate and as he didn't need me to drive him, I took myself out to tea. But excuse me now for a few minutes, will you? Something I have to do in my room——'

Nicola stood up. 'Then I'll go,' she offered.

'No. No, don't, please. Stay. I—I'd like you to meet Kurt. I shan't be long. *Please* stay!' And Diane was gone.

More than a little puzzled by the other girl's manner, Nicola stayed. Several times the lift-gates clanged open and shut, and there was an incessant hum of traffic from the avenue below. But inside the flat the silence was intense and complete, and time lengthened out to a point which at last made nonsense of Diane's 'few minutes' and her 'I shan't be long'.

11

At last Nicola rose and went to listen at the door through which Diane had gone. Nothing to be heard. The door opened on to an inner corridor; there were three doors opposite and one alongside. The latter gave on to a kitchenette; one of the three stood ajar to a bathroom; the other two were closed.

Nicola knocked on one, then opened it. Obviously a man's room—Kurt's. She knocked on the other, called 'Diane, are you there? Are you all right?' in a voice which cracked a little; listened, then opened on to a room as empty of anyone as were all the others.

Diane had left the flat without a hint that she was going! But why? And how? The answer to that one was a further door which led from the room on to the corridor. One of those journeys of the lift had evidently taken Diane down. But why had she suddenly shot off after saying she would be back in the living-room almost at once? She might at least have put her head round the door and given her guest a chance to leave too! Yet she had done neither. Why not?

*Because she hadn't wanted to be questioned.* Because the slight oddness in her manner which Nicola had noticed was somehow connected with this precipitate departure. Only her intuition told Nicola this, but she was pretty sure she was right. Moreover, closer scrutiny of the room showed that Diane had not merely popped down to the nearest *tabac* for cigarettes. The wardrobe was open and empty; there were no toilet things on the surround of the fitted basin; there was no suitcase to be seen (and surely, with yesterday's arrival from Neuchâtel, there ought to be one?). And—Nicola crossed to the bedside table in a couple of strides—there was a letter propped there,

12

addressed to herself.

The writing showed the haste with which it had been written. It read:

'Nicola, you must forgive me. I lied to you. I knew Kurt couldn't be back before you got alarmed and came to look for me. Of course I didn't plan it this way; I couldn't have known that chance would throw us together as it did, but since it has, you've got to help me. Please, Nicola dear! You can, if you will.

'If you know too much, Kurt could be ruthless with you. So I will only say that I *did* plan it—to leave from here, instead of from home, I mean. And to go today, while Kurt was out. When he suggested I should come, I saw that as my chance to get away. I never meant to play hostess for him or whatever—I just made use of the opportunity, that was all.

'Wait for Kurt, please. He may be a long time coming back, but wait and break it to him that I've gone and that this was the only way. He'll guess why, but not where, and you mustn't know either. When I asked you about men this afternoon, I almost confided in you. I'm glad now I didn't. For one thing, you sounded so—sort of detached that you mightn't have understood. But please try now, enough to shield me from Kurt's anger over this.

'I think we've covered our tracks. Kurt mustn't be able to find me—yet. But try to believe, and make Kurt believe it too, that *I'm not doing anything wrong*. Only doing what I must, that's all.

'While we were talking, I took the key to this

13

place off my key-ring. You'll find it on the writing-desk. I shan't need it again. Please let me think, Nicola, that you were *sent* to help me this afternoon. To help Kurt too, perhaps—if he'll let you, which he may not.

Diane.'

Utterly dismayed, torn between indignation and pity, Nicola re-read the letter through, understanding some of it, bewildered by the rest.

'We have covered our tracks.' That meant that, wherever Diane had gone, she hadn't gone alone. Her reference to 'men' told Nicola only one thing. And yet—'I'm not doing anything wrong.' How true was that? Or how much self-deception? And if it were true, what need for Diane to run away from home and her brother's anger at all?

She was *twenty-two*! Her own mistress, surely? Then *why*? And why, for goodness' sake, thought Nicola, off at a tangent of annoyance—why involve *her*; morally tying her hands; forcing her on to Diane's side against this ogre of a brother of whom she seemed to go in fear? What did Diane expect her to do? To say to him? How was she even going to explain to him the how and the why of herself, in place of the sister he would be expecting to see?

Back in the living-room, not knowing how long she must wait, she was almost tempted to pour herself a drink from one of the bottles on a side-table. But she refrained, feeling that for Kurt Thesige to find a stranger quaffing his sherry in his flat would probably not do much for her image.

Much more time passed. There were no books and

she exhausted a couple of glossy magazines quite quickly. More than once she went to the window to see that her car was still where she had parked it, and later she stayed there, looking out and watching the earliest of the city and shop lights come on and, far across the Lake, the lights which were Evian.

Another clanking of the lift and then a key was being used on the outer door. A man came in and, her heart thudding, she turned to face him across the twilit room.

With his left hand—his right wrist was strapped—he flicked a light switch and revealed himself to be tall; as blond as his sister was dark; his features not unlike, but more strongly marked than hers. There was no spare flesh on the bones of his face and premature lines from nostrils to jawbone lent him a maturity that was belied by his lean, athletic body. He was elegantly tailored in lightweight linen and a cream silk shirt. The bulging briefcase which he tossed on to a chair was of mellowed pigskin.

*The complete man-about-town executive, if ever I met one* was Nicola's snap judgment of him as the stare of his grey eyes measured her with cool interest and with less surprise than she expected.

He came over. 'Good evening. I'm sorry—we haven't met, have we? I'm Kurt, of course—— Where is Diane? She didn't say she was expecting anyone. May I offer you a drink, *Mademoiselle*——?'

His use of French took her Swiss nationality for granted, but when she supplied 'Stirling' he frowned quickly and echoed it as a question, giving it its full English sound.

She answered in French. 'Yes, I am English, but I

speak and understand French. And I am a friend—an old friend of Diane's. We met by the oddest chance this afternoon—she left her keys on a café table and I came to return them to this address. But I'm afraid she isn't here now. She left a couple of hours ago, and she—asked me to stay until you came back, *monsieur*.'

Her companion's hand hovered over the bottles. 'Don't you mean until she came back herself?' he queried. 'Where has she gone? Meanwhile, what *aperitif* for you, *mademoiselle*? Sherry, cognac, vodka?'

He hadn't understood! 'Nothing, thank you,' she told him. 'And I did mean "you". Until you returned, that is. Because Diane left, saying she wasn't coming back at all and asking me to stay here long enough to tell you so.'

Kurt Thesige turned then. His puzzled exasperation sparked. 'Not coming back from *where*?'

Nicola shook her head. 'I don't know. She didn't mean I should. Nor you.'

'And you let her go, with no more explanation to yourself or to me than that?'

'I had no choice. After we had talked for a while—oh, I ought to tell you that we knew each other when we were both at Les Cerisiers in Vevey, but hadn't met since—she made an excuse to go to her room, and when she had not reappeared for a long while, I found this'—Nicola handed over Diane's letter—'on her bedside table.'

As she watched Kurt read the letter Nicola wondered whether Diane had meant that he should. But it was too late now. He was looking up from it and quoting.

' "Ruthless." I must say she takes a poor view of my capacity for ordinary courtesy. She doesn't flinch either from making you her catspaw and me her dupe. But what is this about men and your detachment from them? How does that tie in with the rest?'

'Only that she suddenly asked me about any man or men there were in my life, and when I put the same question to her, she evaded it. You see she says there that she almost confided in me, but didn't. And that you would guess her going had to do with some man.'

'As of course I know,' Kurt confirmed shortly. 'Who he is, what he is and how and why he has persuaded her to decamp with him. As for this cant about "nothing wrong"—who does she suppose is going to believe that?'

'It may not be cant. She has underlined it and begs you to believe it. Would she have done that if it weren't true?' Nicola queried.

Kurt dismissed the argument. 'A girl in her state of infatuation can convince herself of anything,' he declared.

'I'd still like to believe it of Diane. Why shouldn't she just have gone away—neither to this man you know about, nor with him?'

'Tch! To him or with him or only because of him, they will fetch up together some time, and because she knows what her friends will conclude, she finds it necessary to protest her innocence and good faith. Just a bromide for her conscience, that's all.'

Nicola persisted, 'But why should she have to run away? Or justify her actions to you? I know her age, because she is three years younger than I am, and——'

Kurt confirmed, 'Yes, twenty-two, and legally of age. But she happens to be in a special relationship to me, that's why. Financially and for permission to marry before she is twenty-five, her father's will made her dependent on me. In her last year at Vevey she had a silly affair with another man—but if you knew her then, you may have known about that?'

'No. I was teaching English there and I left a year before she did.'

'So? Well, in consequence of that escapade, Father —who, I may say, made this one of the few business matters he entrusted to me—made me the guarantor against a repetition of the same thing, by ensuring that she wouldn't be at the mercy of the next fortune-hunting type who happened along. Now she is of age she might be successful in getting the clause revoked. But no—she prefers to try a private moral blackmail of me instead. Well, we shall see, Mademoiselle Diane and Monsieur Anton Pellerin the garage-hand, shall we not?' Kurt challenged sourly.

In face of his lack of it, Nicola felt sympathy for Diane thrust upon her. 'You mean,' she said, 'you know this man—the present one—to be a fortune-hunter too?'

Kurt shrugged. 'What else? He works—or did until a week ago—at the garage we use in Neuchâtel. He taught her to drive. It's the classic situation brought up to date. The nineteenth-century demoiselle fell for her riding instructor or her violin master and *my* sister goes down for a garage mechanic with a shrewd eye to a Thesige alliance and an attractive bride thrown in!'

18

'And you know for sure that this Anton Pellerin isn't working at your garage any more?'

'I heard it by chance and was glad, thinking, "Well, that's that." I haven't been in Diane's confidence about the affair, and I was equally glad when she jumped at my suggestion she should come to Lausanne as my social hostess. Temporarily as my chauffeur too——' Kurt gestured towards his wrist.

Nicola said, 'Yes, she told me. That she made use of the chance to leave from here instead of from home. She rather made use of me too, didn't she? I—I'm sorry, *monsieur*. But you do see there was nothing I could do?'

'Nothing. Think nothing of it. I ought to thank you,' he said.

'For what?'

'Well, at least for your misguided loyalty to Diane.'

'That was easy. We were friends,' Nicola said simply.

He looked at her sharply. 'You mean that as a rebuke for my much more cynical view of the scene?'

Nicola picked up her bag, preparatory to leaving. 'I've no right to rebuke you, *monsieur*,' she said.

'But you would like to.' He made it a statement. 'You also badly want to know what happens next; what I intend to do in the matter.'

Nicola faced him, standing. 'Isn't that natural? Even though I didn't ask to be involved?'

'Very natural, and I'd have told you anyway. So, regarding any immediate hue-and-cry for Diane wherever she is, nothing. For the rest——'

'Nothing?'

'*Nothing?*'

He ignored the shock in Nicola's tone. 'For the moment, no. Whatever is done, is done. In my own good time I shall take steps, but if a waiting game to test my reaction is what my sister wants, then a waiting game she shall have. Meanwhile, I admit, I'm as much concerned with my immediate embarrassment. I had a use for Diane during my sales campaign here. But I gather I can't look for your sympathy over that?'

Nicola said slowly, 'If I'm honest, I'd have more if you showed more concern about Diane.'

'And you're honest to a fault, aren't you? And a better friend than she deserves.'

That was too much. Nicola exploded, 'How can you say that? What do you suppose it must have cost Diane to do this? Even leaving your business plans in the lurch couldn't have been easy. You don't seem to have any pity. Besides, you can't just do "nothing" to find her! Her aunt—yours—in Neuchâtel will have to know.'

Unmoved, Kurt said, 'For the moment, there is no reason why she should. When we came to Lausanne, she took the opportunity to go to stay with friends in Paris. No, until I decide so, there is no need for her to know. Since Diane didn't worry about her, I must, and not to alarm her yet is the best way.'

Nicola sighed and tucked her bag under her arm. 'I'm sorry. You apparently have everything in control——' she began.

'But I haven't.' With a couple of steps he effectually barred her way to the door. 'There's still my lack of a hostess for my business guests.'

'Which I hope very much you will solve.'

His lips stretched in a faint smile. 'Your tone implies you don't think I deserve to! However, if you're leaving, may I call a cab and drop you at your hotel? Or aren't you on holiday, perhaps? Do you live here?'

'No. I'm staying at a *pension* on the Avenue Kléber and I shall be here for a week or two more. But I have a hired car. It's parked outside.'

'Then you are on holiday?'

'For the rest of my time, yes.' As he waited for her to enlarge on that, she told him briefly about her circumstances and her plan to spend the proceeds of her late job in Lausanne and its surroundings.

'A pity about Diane,' he commented. 'You might have seen something of each other while you were here.'

She agreed, 'Yes, I'd have liked that, and I suggested as much to Diane, but——'

'You wouldn't consider me as a substitute companion? Say for dinner tonight, perhaps?'

'I——'

He read into her hesitation the refusal she intended. 'No?' he parried. 'I'm still in disgrace? But at least a cognac before you go?' Giving her no chance to say No to that, he poured two and handed one glass to her.

As she sat down again reluctantly, he went on, 'I suppose it doesn't occur to you that if you are as deeply concerned as you seem, your best chance of news of Diane is not to lose all touch with me?'

'I'll give you my full address, *monsieur*, and I hope very much you will let me know as soon as you hear anything about her,' Nicola said quietly.

'But of course. Meanwhile'—he paused for a long while, twirling the stem of his glass—'meanwhile it occurs to *me* that you could be in a position to help both Diane and myself—if you would.'

Nicola looked up. 'If *I* would? I don't understand?'

For the first time the smile he gave her held apology; he momentarily lost arrogance, disarming her. He shrugged. 'No details offer themselves. Just an idea——'

'An idea about what?'

She had to wait for his reply to that. When it came —'Scandal,' he said bluntly. 'The averting of. By means of a combined operation between my expertise and your goodwill. It's just possible that, working together, we might beat this problem.'

'You mean—finding Diane before she has done anything—very rash?'

He shook his head. 'I doubt if that's possible, considering that "we" in her letter. It implies that she and Pellerin have teamed up, hoping that in some village of some *canton* or other they may be able to persuade a *curé* that they are free to marry. No, I meant really that, with you to feather the shaft, I might be able to save her from the worst of the scandal she'll invite until she is found——' He broke off at Nicola's puzzled glance his way. 'Oh, you don't understand me? You haven't the expression "to feather the shaft" in English?'

'I don't think so. I've never heard it.'

'But you have—let us see—to "lend a hand"? To "back up"? Well, instead, we draw on the parallel of our Swiss bowmen, who used to rely on their squires to fit the flight feathers to their arrows for them. Just a phrase—no more—to express what you might do to help Diane if you would.'

'I see. And that would be?' Nicola invited non-committally.

'To——' He paused, holding her glance. 'To—you make this very difficult, *mademoiselle*!—to take her place until she is found or shows her hand. In other words, to play stand-in for her, which is a phrase I'm sure you do know?'

Nicola stared at him. 'Of course I do, though I've no idea what you mean by it in this case. How could I possibly take Diane's place—in any capacity at all?'

'Why not?' His manner assured again, he sat easily on the arm of a chair. 'For instance, and step by step—— You drive a car. You could play my chauffeur for the short time I'm unable to be my own. Your French is excellent; your English is your own and you say that, like Diane, you have some Italian too. Fortunately your English would be most in demand in your nursing along of the womenfolk of my business contact types. Interpreting for them, acting as their social bridge while they and their men are here, playing my hostess to them on occasion—it's a role I judge you could move on to with ease, from what you have told me about your late job with your English trade delegation. So I repeat—why not?'

Nicola let him finish. Then she said slowly, 'May I get this clear? You're suggesting that I should take on all that Diane would have done for you if she had stayed?'

He nodded. 'For a suitable fee, of course.'

'For "a suitable fee" you could hire a chauffeur or take a cab, couldn't you?'

'True, I could. It's a small point.'

'And no doubt you could hire the services of a professional social hostess for your entertaining?'

'There—no. I am a single man and you'll probably appreciate that my employment of a professional hostess might have—shall we call them—damaging overtones?'

His meaning was not lost on Nicola and she flushed. 'Some friend, then?' she persisted. 'Some married or older friend who would help you out? You must know someone who would!'

'But of course. Except that, unless she were some dowager of eighty or so, the same delicate situation would arise. What's more, once I appeal to just one woman friend, the news of Diane's defection will be out. And in my own interests just now, as well as hers, this I can't afford.'

Nicola frowned, groping for a thread of argument which eluded her. Finding it, 'I'm afraid you don't make yourself at all clear, *monsieur*,' she told him. 'I don't understand you. For if I agreed to stand in for Diane as you suggest, you would be making *me* your professional hostess. And once I appeared anywhere with you in that role, the news about Diane *must* come out!'

He didn't reply. He gestured towards her glass and when she shook her head, he turned to refill his own. With his back to her—'Not,' he said, 'if you and I were the only people to know it was a business arrangement between us. So there would be no sidelong glances; no cause for wagging tongues. And certainly not, if we made your proxy role the total one I envisage for you —that of your *being*, so far as all these strangers and foreigners are concerned, the young, attractive, trilingual sister I have brought with me to Lausanne to help with their entertainment while they and I do business together——'

He broke off and turned then. 'You see? I make myself clear now?'

Almost doubting her hearing, Nicola assured him, 'You do indeed. And you must be equally clear as to what my answer is?'

'But naturally. In the light of cold reason, what else could you make it than No?'

Oddly, his easy agreement once again disarmed her. But she handed him her empty glass and stood up. 'Well, as long as that is understood——'

'Ah, but in *less* than cold reason?' he cut in. 'For no other reason, in fact, than for Diane's sake, for her Aunt Agathe's, for the sake of anyone who cares for her? Even—though this won't count with you—for mine?'

'But how could my impersonation of Diane possibly do a thing to help any of you?'

'Because we are Thesiges, which makes us public gossip-fodder, whether we like it or not. We go about our lawful occasions normally and without incident, and we are let alone. But once invite a headline like— "Thesige Chief, on trade mission in Lausanne, reports unexplained disappearance of his sister, Mademoiselle Diane Thesige"—and it will blow up into a scandal that will touch us all. Whereas, if my sister can be *seen* to be among those present, acting as my hostess——'

'But if you are as well known as that, surely——?' Nicola broke off; the enormity of the thing was too much to grasp.

Kurt was swift to pounce on her hesitancy. 'I've told you—the details elude me. And since their success must stand or fall by you, at least give me an hour to work on them and then allow me to put them to you over dinner?'

Nicola shook her head. 'It's a wild, impossible scheme.'

'But if I could show it to be not so impossible? Not so wild? You might consider it—in order to shield Diane?'

As he saw she was on her way to the door, he put down his refilled glass, the cognac untouched, and went with her. He opened the door for her, ignoring the hand she held out to him. 'I'll see you to your car.'

He did so in silence. But when she had taken her seat and was about to switch on, then he offered his hand. Holding hers in a firm cool grasp, 'You promised to give me the address of your *pension* on the Avenue Kléber?' he said.

'Yes. It is Number Sixteen. The district is——'

'I know the district. So I shall call for you there at'—he looked at his watch—'say, eight-thirty?—and we shall go somewhere to dine.'

Without giving her a chance to accept or refuse, he turned on his heel and left her.

# CHAPTER TWO

LATE that night, still in the light silk coat she had worn for the evening, Nicola sat before her dressing-table mirror, asking in a whisper of her reflection, 'What have I done? What *have* I done?'

Her thoughts ranged back, in search of the points at which she might have said No to Kurt Thesige—but had not.

It should have been easy, when he called for her, to make her refusal to dine with him a No of which he could hardly have mistaken the finality. But when she had gone to meet him in the hall of the *pension*, her fellow guests had been milling there in answer to the summons of the dinner-gong, and without giving her a chance to protest, Kurt's hand had been beneath her elbow, propelling her into the taxi he had asked to wait.

Without consulting her choice, he had taken her to a quiet restaurant on the Avenue de Cour and, committed at least to dining with him, she had had no early opportunity to say No to a matter which he seemed in no hurry to bring up.

Instead, over the meal, he had put to her the kind of questions any interested companion had a right to ask. More about her work than she had previously told him; about her languages, and something of her personal background. She told him that, between assignments, she lived in a hostel in London; she was an

27

only child; her father was dead and her mother, re-married, had gone with her new husband to Cyprus. During that recital only Kurt's question as to how much she knew or remembered of Lausanne's surroundings had any bearing on their earlier talk. They had reached the dessert course and she had begun to wonder whether he had had second thoughts; whether his entertainment of her was no more than an invitation to dinner of Diane's friend, when his abrupt, significant, 'Well?' had offered the chance of a No which she had not taken.

Instead she had temporised, sensing that he would scorn to persuade her further if she refused outright. And if she were honest, she knew she wanted to explore any possibility of helping Diane. So, just in case he *was* thinking of Diane's good name, she had told him, 'I hope you'll take it that I'd give a lot to save Diane from scandal. But what you suggested this afternoon seems to me so unworkable that I can't see how you could expect me to agree to it.'

'But I didn't ask you to agree with it, sight unseen. I only asked you to consider it in the light of my ability to make it workable—always supposing I could,' he had retorted, once again destroying her argument by admitting her right to make it, and had gone on to remind her, 'And if you weren't prepared to give me a hearing, you wouldn't have joined me tonight.'

'You gave me very little choice,' she had reminded him in her turn.

'Enough, surely? Short of a forcible kidnapping, a woman always has weapons of refusal to her hand. And since you didn't send a message to me from your

28

room and you did come, will you at least listen while I outline the thing for you; deal with the difficulties I've foreseen and try to show you that it could work, if you would let it?'

To that she had agreed, 'Of course I am willing to listen.'

'Then do, please.' Whereupon he had proceeded to marshal obstacle after obstacle, most of them of his thinking, but some, with uncanny insight, of hers—to mount them and then demolish them one by one with such a laying-waste of further argument against, that, an hour later, she had been scarcely surprised to hear herself saying Yes to him, and only now that she was alone again was she aghast at her folly.

Yet at the time he had so convinced her her agreement was no folly but reasonable and necessary—promising the only way open to her of gaining valuable time for Diane—time for the girl to think again; to make a move, to regret, or to stand her ground, untouched by the scandal she had invited by her flight; scandal she perhaps deserved ... perhaps did not.

So Nicola had listened ... even made her own suggestions ... helped Kurt's scheme along. How had he hypnotised her so? (How willing *was* the victim to be hypnotised by the basilisk's stare?) Or—a hopeful thought this—was he right, and she wrong to doubt that he was? At that point she knew she had to review his arguments, looking for the flaws that might spell her right to escape ... Always supposing she wanted to escape, so throwing Diane to the lions of malicious gossip and worse.

And so—— Kurt had brought no personal staff

with him and now would call none from Neuchâtel to join him. He had always intended to use the services of a temporary secretary from the Lausanne pool. For the two days of his exhibition at the Palais de Beaulieu, when his Neuchâtel-based salesmen must man the stands, Nicola need not appear; likewise, when the visiting delegations of buyers were taken to his factories, Nicola could stay behind with the women guests of the party.

There would be the inevitable press stories and photographs at functions. But the latter were notoriously vague with individual detail, and Nicola, as dark and youthful-looking as Diane, would almost certainly pass for the latter. None of his expected guests had ever met Diane, and, so far as he knew, she had no friends in Lausanne. And—here forestalling Nicola's as yet unspoken question—she need not worry that she would be put in any intolerable situation with regard to himself. As sister and brother, he and Diane would have needed no chaperonage in their quarters. But Nicola, not being in fact Diane, must have her position protected. Which made it as well that the flat from which Diane had left was merely a couple of nights' stand for them. The furnished villa he had rented for the period of his entertaining would be ready and fully manned tomorrow by a married Italian couple whom he had met only at one interview and who had never seen Diane at all.

So far as he could foresee, there would be no one in a position to question the relationship, and though difficulties might arise, they must be dealt with at the time and on their merits. Obviously they could not all be forestalled in advance ... Finally, as the nature of the job was more than a shade unusual, he would prefer that Nicola named her own fee. Perhaps it would be as well if she did not arrive at a figure until she had experienced what the assignment asked of her, but in the meanwhile anything she needed for the forwarding of her role should be bought in his name; he would see that the necessary credit cards were forthcoming. She would regard such an arrangement as satisfactory?

There were no flaws. She could not but admire his grasp of and cold, impersonal disposal of each problem in turn; his assumption that they both understood it was merely a temporary job they were discussing; that there was no question of his asking a personal favour of her. And now, looking back over the evening, Nicola knew that it was that detachment on his part which had made possible her Yes to him. What was more, appalled and in sore doubt of its wisdom though she was, she was subtly aware that she might have regretted a No as much. For, unlike him, she could not approach the thing wholly impersonally. He had *expected* her to agree for Diane's sake; to refuse would have been a betrayal of Diane and more. Somehow her own pride would have suffered in face of Kurt Thesige's confidence in her power to help Diane ... to help him, supposing she had said No.

The next morning she settled her bill with the *pension*, returned her hired car to the garage, packed and was ready for Kurt when he called for her in the afternoon by taxi.

As the porter carried out her luggage she saw Kurt glance at it. 'It's as well it's not initialled,' he approved. 'Otherwise it would have had to go into store.' And in the taxi he said, 'I'm trusting you to keep any personal papers which show your name— your passport, for instance—under lock and key. And one other thing that I took as read last night but haven't mentioned yet. To all intents I am your brother. Therefore I am always "Kurt" to you. And, as the Lost Pets columns put it, you will have to "answer to" Diane's name. Will you remember that?'

Nicola looked away out of the taxi window. 'I shall have to try, shan't I?' she said.

'I hope you'll do better than try,' he retorted. 'You must school yourself to respond every time. To the "Mademoiselle Thesige" of other people too——' He paused for a long time and then, as if calling her attention to something, uttered a sharp 'Diane!'

Nicola turned her head at once. She saw him smile. 'Good. An excellent reflex that time. Keep it up,' he said.

He had directed the taxi to the Avenue d'Elysée where his rented villa stood dwarfed by the old-fashioned, many-floored mansions on its either side. It was hidden from view by a wall behind which the sound of the endless sweep of cars on the Avenue was muted. It was stuccoed cream with grey shutters to the windows and a grey pantiled roof. It was modern and inviting and justified its name of La Villa des Figuiers by the trained fig-trees which spread formally over its side walls.

There was a garage, its slide-over door open to the sun, where there stood a big car of Italian make. Kurt nodded towards it. 'Our transport, when we are going anywhere together. But I thought it more discreet to

32

fetch you from your *pension* by taxi,' he remarked, leaving Nicola to wonder, with a sense of chill, how often in the coming days the word 'discreet' would be exchanged between them.

Signora Ralli, middle-aged and plump, was at the door to greet them. Her husband carried Nicola's luggage to her room and Kurt introduced her, 'Signorina Thesige, my sister. You will find she speaks better Italian than I do,' before asking for tea to be brought to them in the pleasant salon as soon as Nicola came downstairs again.

When she did so he was sorting through some papers in his briefcase. 'Do you like your room?' he asked over his shoulder.

'Yes, it's charming.'

'Well, don't hesitate to ask either of the Rallis for anything you need. And by the way'—he passed to her a driving licence—'Diane obligingly left that behind. I found it in her room at the flat. You'd better keep it in your bag.'

Nicola fingered it doubtfully. 'But I have one of my own!'

'Which must be put aside with your passport. Nor must you drive on Diane's.'

'Then why give it to me?'

'Only as an additional piece of cover for you in case you need it. No, I've had to rethink on your role as my chauffeur, even temporarily. We can't risk the slightest brush with the police. But I find Ralli can drive, so when we aren't together he can drive you or you must take a cab. And my wrist is up to the job now, though I'll keep it strapped for a few days more.'

He next took a wallet from his case. 'There's this

too. You'll need some ready money, no doubt.'

'I don't. I have enough, thank you.'

'Of your own. Yes, so you said last night. But this is an advance on your fee.' As she still did not take the wallet from him, he snapped open the clasp of her bag and thrust it inside. 'Don't worry. I'm a businessman. I know just how much I'm giving you and you're going to earn it and more—I hope,' he said drily. 'And now what about some tea?'

Over it he told her that some of his clients were already staying in various hotels in the city. 'I've invited a few for drinks this evening at the Lausanne-Palace. Do you know it?' he asked.

She shook her head. 'Only from the outside. I'm afraid my budget is more in the *pension* and café-bar bracket.'

He sent her a swift critical look. 'And that's the kind of honesty you can't afford as a genuine Thesige,' he commented.

Nicola flushed. 'I'm sorry.'

He smiled then, 'My fault. I handed it to you on a plate. So we've *both* got to be careful,' he said, once again turning the edge of the argument against himself ... meeting her halfway.

Meanwhile there was a question she had to ask. 'About Diane,' she said a little later. 'You weren't serious when you said you intended to do nothing to find her? Because there must surely be some steps you could take?'

He set down his cup and lit a cigarette. 'Such as the police, the press, private detection, a set of sandwich-boards or the town crier? Which would you recommend?' he parried.

34

She flinched at an irony for which she hadn't been prepared. 'That's not fair of you. I only thought——'

'Then don't,' advised Kurt. He stood, picked up his briefcase and passing her chair on his way from the room, laid a hand briefly on her shoulder. 'That part of this problem is my concern, not yours, and if you remember, I told you I'd take steps to solve it when I see fit; steps I may not choose to share with you. In the meanwhile, let's leave it on the table—may we?'

The last two words were neither a question nor an appeal. They were a demand for her agreement which went no way at all to meet her. What a baffling man he was! And for a rare glimpse of the candour and self-criticism that lent him a certain charm, what a price in domination and arrogance he asked!

While she changed in readiness for Kurt's cocktail party Nicola tried consciously to learn her part; to make herself over into Diane as an actress must; to begin to think in French instead of in English—which her flair for the language never found difficult—and to remember as her own recent history all that she had learned of Diane's doings during their hour of talk in the flat.

It was as well, she felt, that both she and Kurt would be moving among strangers to them both, for there was no question of achieving any close physical resemblance to Diane, who was not as tall, who wore her hair longer and used more emphasised make-up. But Nicola faithfully obeyed orders; locking away her passport, destroying letters from England and unpicking telltale English labels from her clothes. She turned out her handbag; put Diane's driving licence into her wallet and substituted for her English-made compact and lipstick a Swiss set she had bought only the day before. To wear for the evening she chose an Italian silk cowl-necked dress with a swing to it which had been an extravagance of her holiday in Venice last year and which, from the small selection on offer in her wardrobe, it was easy to guess would have been Diane's choice.

She was tingling with apprehension when she went down to Kurt, awaiting her in the salon. He looked her over. 'Yes,' he said, which might mean anything, then gestured to her left wrist. 'No watch?' he asked.

She glanced down. 'Yes. But it's rather workaday—and English, so I left it off.'

'If you hadn't, I'd have asked you to.' As he spoke he took from his breast pocket a jewellers' case scrawled in gilt lettering 'Thesige'. He handed it to her with a smile. 'Not good for our image for you to be wearing anything but the home product. Put it on,' he said.

'Oh!' Her gasp of admiration was for the exquisite little gold bracelet-watch which was bedded on the velvet of the case. 'It—it's quite lovely. Do you mean —you are lending it to me?'

'Lending it? My dear girl, Thesige isn't in the hire business! Naturally I'm giving it to you—what do you suppose? Come——'

As she hadn't picked it up, he did so for her, turned her wrist inwards to him and bent over the clasp of the bracelet. The fastening completed, he continued to hold her hand by the fingers for a moment, his touch as cool and impersonal as a formal handshake. Impossible to see the gift as anything other than an additional setting for her role. But what a pity, was her half-caught thought, that such a lovely thing should mean no more to either giver or receiver than that!

A few minutes later they set out in the car, Kurt driving. The city and the lakeside boulevards were aglow with light; the surface of the Lake itself throwing back its reflection in long, shimmering paths. As they entered the foyer of the great hotel Nicola had time to wonder what she would have been doing if she were not here. Probably scanning the evening paper for a French film to see after the first sitting for dinner at the *pension*, came the answer. Then she and Kurt Thesige were part of the *luxe* surrounding them; the cosmopolitan feel of the place, the perfumed air, the hubbub of half a dozen spoken tongues and the smoothly geared service which wealth commanded.

Kurt guided Nicola to a lounge marked on its door 'Reserved for the party of Monsieur Thesige', and two or three of his guests were already there. When they were all assembled there were a couple of Italians, some Americans accompanied by their wives, a young German whose English was better than his French and for the rest, some Frenchmen and two English buyers from the Midlands.

Nicola was introduced to them all in turn as 'My sister, Diane. She knows I brought her along to be useful as well as ornamental. So please ask her anything you want to know. Because that's what she is here for—to do the honours of the place.'

Upon which one of the American matrons beamed upon Nicola, 'Does that mean you're going to be a kind of courier to us, dear? How real cosy!' causing Kurt to murmur under his breath to Nicola, 'Sounds as if you may have to learn to refuse a tip gracefully!' and then with a private smile that she found warming, 'You're making a success so far. I'm proud of you.'

In fact, the strangers' unquestioning acceptance of her made things much easier than she had feared. By the time the party was ready to break up she was almost completely at ease. It was at that point, when the Americans had already gone and Kurt was engaged with the Englishmen that the young German, Hans Durer, came over to her as she stood alone.

He said in his careful English, 'It is true, *mademoiselle*, that you are to be your brother's hostess to us while we are here?'

She smiled at him, liking his frank blue eyes, his freckles and his springing red hair. 'Yes, Herr Durer,' she told him. 'I'm looking forward to it. How long are you staying in Lausanne?'

'I came just for the Palais de Beaulieu Exhibition, and I may stay only for its first day.'

'You are from Düsseldorf, aren't you?'

'Yes. My brother and I have our own business on the Rosenstrasse. Do you know Düsseldorf, *mademoiselle*?'

'No.' She was on firm ground here. Diane had mentioned that she had only been to Hanover and West Berlin.

'It's a fine city. I should like to show it to you. Meanwhile,' he hesitated, 'as I am alone in my hotel here, I am wondering if you could find time to lunch with me? Tomorrow perhaps, if you are free?'

'Oh. Thank you. I'd like that—some time.'

'But not tomorrow?'

'Well, I think not. You see, I don't know what my

38

brother's plans are for me,' Nicola said, pretty sure that a tête-à-tête luncheon so early in her role was not among them.

Hans Durer took the rebuff with good grace. 'But another time? I may ask you again? I am at the Hotel Lac Bleu near the University. Not quite five-star, you understand, but a pleasant place.' He bowed then and left her and went to take his leave of Kurt. The two Englishmen left with him and then she and Kurt were alone.

He came across to her. 'I've made a date for you to meet the ladies for coffee at the Salon Manuel tomorrow at eleven,' he told her. 'And now, would you like to stay here for dinner, or shall we drive somewhere else?'

Nicola glanced at his wrist. 'Do you want to drive any further?'

'Yes, I'm quite able. There's a small place on the Lake between here and Morges, where they serve a good *raclette* and superb lake trout. We'll go there.'

Beyond the city boundaries the road was bordered by linden trees in fresh bud, and in the darkness the magnolia blossom in the villa gardens glowed like white lamps. Their destination was a small lakeside *brasserie*, where most of the patrons arrived by scooter or on foot, where Madame was the chef and Monsieur both head-waiter and barman and where the excellent homely meal was served on checked gingham place-clothes on an extension of the bar.

While they ate Kurt offered thumbnail sketches of the people they had met, and Nicola asked what she should do with the next morning's party after coffee.

'M'm——' he considered. 'You might suggest an

39

afternoon's drive to the narcissus fields at Les Avants, though I rather think they'd prefer a guided tour round the shops. By the way, has anyone remarked on your command of English?'

'I've been congratulated on it.'

He laughed shortly. 'Which you must have found ironic. What were you speaking with young Durer?'

'English. He asked me to have luncheon with him tomorrow. I put him off because I didn't know what your plans for me were. But I think he will ask me again. If he does, may I accept?'

'Do you want to accept?'

Nicola said carefully, 'He seems pleasant, and it would be rude to continue to refuse without reason.'

'As you say—— Then do accept. But don't encourage him.'

'Encourage him in what?'

Kurt's eyes narrowed. 'You know perfectly well what I mean. Also why it wouldn't do. Or must I remind you that, to all intents, you are Diane Thesige, not Nicola Stirling on a business assignment?'

'And he sells watches and clocks and barometers in Düsseldorf, which doesn't rate him very differently from a garage-hand in Neuchâtel? No, you needn't remind me. I understand perfectly now why he is not to be "encouraged".'

Nicola made a quotation of the word and saw Kurt flinch with anger. 'That sounds deliberately offensive,' he said, his tone barely controlled. He waited, as if for her apology, and when she said nothing, he went on:

'So you meant it to be. You resented the implication that you couldn't control the early stages of an affair, so you had to hit back. Unfairly, as it happens. There

40

was no comparison in my mind between Hans Durer and Anton Pellerin. All I meant in warning you was concern for Durer himself. For example, consider the effect on him of falling for and being encouraged by a willing girl, only for her to disappear like Cinderella at midnight. As you must, you'll agree, when the midnight of *our* private arrangement strikes?'

She felt shamed and at the same time oddly chilled by the logic of his argument. A Cinderella. Yes, at the end of all this, that's what she would be. A Cinderella —and no glass slipper of recall for her . . . She told him quietly, 'I see. I'm sorry, I misunderstood you, I'm afraid.'

'You did indeed, and our relationship can't afford cross-purposes. However'—his shrug abandoned the argument—'would you care to dance?'

Still gauche after his reproof and shy of close contact with him while she felt so, she said, 'I don't think so, thank you'—only to realise, to her further chagrin, that he wasn't offering to partner her himself.

Instead he nodded at the mirror they faced across the bar-counter. 'No? I asked because that youth in the velvet jacket has been eyeing your back and your profile, whenever you have offered it to him, for quite some time. One full turn of the head and the ghost of a smile for him, and he'll be over here at a bound and, romance-wise, at your feet.'

Nicola looked into the mirror and saw the lanky teenager draped against the curtained archway which led to a further room where a few couples drifted and gyrated and occasionally clapped to demand more music from the unseen player of an accordion.

'Then I'll be careful not to turn and not to smile.

41

I'd rather not dance tonight,' she said, and again heard Kurt's short laugh.

'Determined to show you can take men or leave them at will? Is that what Diane meant by your "detachment" from them, in her letter to you?' he asked.

She felt her colour rise. 'I don't know. She only asked me quite suddenly what about any men in my life—possibly, I've thought since, because she was on the verge of telling me about her own affair. I said that naturally there had been some men for me since we last met. But she didn't confide in me and she changed the subject without asking me whether there was anyone for me now.'

'And is there?'

Nicola didn't answer the bluntness of that directly. 'If Diane had asked me, I'd have told her No,' she said. 'But even if I haven't any loyalties anywhere else, I still shan't embarrass you with any of your associates while I'm standing in for her.'

'As I guessed, you are very sure, aren't you, of your power to keep my sex at its distance?' he taunted lightly.

'Well, wasn't that what you were asking of me just now? That I shouldn't get involved?'

'True,' Kurt agreed, 'before I realised how well in hand your emotions are. For instance, you dismiss these previous and plural affairs of yours without the flinch of an eyelid! No scars inflicted or sustained?'

'Scars don't last for ever.'

'With which women can usually salve their consciences when it was their finger on the trigger. Poor Velvet Jacket now! You looked, you measured; he never had a hope, but did you care? Young Durer too

42

—if he starts anything, you'll cope. This poise! This English *sangfroid*! No wonder it numbed Diane's impulse to confide her silly infatuation to you! Tell me, do they teach it to you in your cradles, or at finishing school, or where?'

She was taken unawares by this broadside attack. 'Now you are generalising and jumping to conclusions too,' she said. 'If we have it, I suppose we learn it from experience and in self-defence. But I doubt if any of us would claim we have enough to deal with every situation.'

Kurt signalled to Monsieur for his bill and paid it before he replied. Then, as he handed her down from her stool, he asked, 'But you'd say you have enough for handling the present emergency?'

'I—hope so.'

On their way out Nicola realised she had made that slight hesitation a kind of talisman for herself; a guarded finger-crossing against the fear that in some crises the emergency might throw up, her detachment might prove sadly lacking. And in the car, tensely aware of the man beside her and of his demands upon her, she found herself wondering where her earlier confidence of the evening had gone.

## CHAPTER THREE

DURING the next few days Nicola saw little of Kurt, who worked with his temporary secretary in the mornings and divided the rest of his time between the telephone and long sessions at the Palais de Beaulieu, the international convention centre. Each morning too he briefed Nicola on any new guests who had arrived in Lausanne overnight; after which she rang their hotels and introduced herself and suggested a meeting for morning coffee with any ladies of the party, or a morning lake tour or a drive out to one of the neighbouring vineyards and its wine-tasting cellars.

She was always welcomed. The Americans especially seemed naïvely pleased to find their informal entertainment laid on for them, and though Kurt's fear that she might be offered a tip proved groundless, their kindness pressed many gifts on her—flowers and perfume and offer upon offer to 'visit with us in the States. Just stop by any time, honey, and you'll find us at home to you.'

She was touched, awed and guilty by turn, the guilt of her deception often waking her suddenly and disastrously in the small hours but having to be resolutely smothered by day. She had to *be* Diane; *had* to be! she warned herself fiercely. And was—successfully— with these kindly strangers she was deluding, but never for a moment in her thoughts of Kurt, nor in his company, with other people there too. Then she had to struggle painfully to play his sister, and though the effect might be the same, her mind always denied it.

She was Nicola Stirling ... English ... a stranger, and nothing to a man named Kurt Thesige—nothing. And he—nothing to her. Just her employer in a bizarre freak of a job, nothing more. (Why had that thought begun to hurt?)

The fine spell held; the sun's warmth strengthened; the lidos on the lake-front down at Ouchy were gay with sun-umbrellas on their terraces and riotous with happy noise in their sparkling pools. A favourite lido with the Thesige party was La Harpe de Bellerive, and it was there that Kurt and Nicola drove one morning when he said he was free until lunchtime and would enjoy a swim.

Other people joined them. Nicola swam with Hans Durer who, until then, hadn't renewed his invitation, but did so by asking her to dinner that evening.

This time she accepted. 'I'll look forward to it. Where shall I come? To the Lac Bleu?' she asked.

'No. I'll hire a car and call for you and we'll drive out somewhere. Perhaps to Vevey, I thought. Didn't you tell me you were at school there?'

'I didn't. My brother may have mentioned it. But yes, I was there about four or five years ago.'

'Four or five years? *So* long ago?' Hans shook his head in disbelief. 'No, you cannot possibly have been old enough to leave school then!' he claimed.

Nicola laughed. 'But I was, and I did.' She added with truth of her own school-leaving, 'I was eighteen, so why do you doubt it? Am I as gauche as all that?'

'Gauche! *Gauche, mademoiselle?*' His blue eyes started with horror. 'You can't possibly think——!

You must know I meant a compliment—that to me you seem so young, so—fresh, so untouched that I——'

He broke off awkwardly and Nicola looked away, angry with herself for the silly, arch taunt which had provoked his outburst. Kurt had warned her against 'encouraging' Hans, and her coy question to him had done just that. She was relieved when, after a moment of silence, he asked more levelly:

'And since then you have lived at home, and gone abroad often and been gay?'

She chose the part of the question which she could answer with truth. 'Yes, I've been abroad quite a lot. To Italy, and to Paris, and Scotland and Cyprus——'

'You must know England too? You speak the language so well.'

'So do you,' she smiled at him.

He looked pleased. 'You think so? I am glad. For if I did not, how should we communicate, when my French is—*ach!*'—his downturned thumb was expressive—'and my Italian is worse?'

They had been sitting on the pool edge, dabbling their toes, but now he sprang up, offering her a hand. 'Now we will dive again, and then go to the bar for a long, cool drink?'

She allowed him to pull her to her feet and she took off her sunglasses. But as she stooped to lay them on her towel, she was aware of Kurt a few yards away. He stood alone, one thumb hooked into the belt of his swimming trunks, the other hand shading his eyes against the sun which, for Nicola, made only a figure in silhouette of the woman who was approaching him, both arms theatrically outstretched.

She greeted him in a voice so husky as to have almost a masculine depth, 'Kurt! Kurt *Thesige*! After all this time! Our summer at Antibes—do you remember? But no, why should you? I know very well that you forgot *me* soon enough!' The words came across to Nicola in English with a faintly foreign inflection she could not place. She saw Kurt's start of recognition but did not hear his reply, so urgently did she drop to her knees on her towel and crouch there, face hidden from them, in an instinctive effort to hide.

She felt the prickle of sheer panic at the roots of her hair; gooseflesh along her spine. Someone who knew Kurt! Who knew him well enough to greet him teasingly and by his first name! Who, almost certainly, knew Diane too—the real Diane. And so became the one chance that Kurt had risked—the chance which seemingly had now happened. As if, thought Nicola, her shock only too ready to blame him, he oughtn't to have foreseen that it might!

She looked round over her shoulder. Hans had moved away to the edge of the pool and was waiting for her. She thought neither Kurt nor the stranger had seen her, but she answered Hans's beckoning by crawling on all fours towards him, stood for only a split second before her dive and, after it, swam under water to the furthest point of the pool.

Hans came up beside her. 'Shall we go for our drink now?' he asked.

'Not yet. I'm enjoying this.' She swam away from him towards another group of swimmers. Among so many bobbing heads there was safety for a time. But of course it was only a ruse; she couldn't stay anonymously in the pool for ever. And when she came out,

47

what then?

Treading water and floating, she looked back at Kurt and the woman, seeing her plainly now. She was very slim and tall; her graceful legs, and her arms and shoulders above her brief halter-top, a deep golden bronze which she could not have acquired during the week of spring sunshine which Lausanne had enjoyed so far, after a longer spell of chilly winds from the north. Her hair, fashionably unkempt, was as blonde as Kurt's but with a broad, silver-white streak springing back from her brow. Her face, now in profile to Nicola, was slightly gaunt, the nose aquiline, the lips rather a thin line. She had spoken to Kurt in English, but talking to him now, the expressive use of her hands and eyes was un-English. When she laughed in her deep husky voice, heads turned her way, and Kurt, listening and replying, was intent upon her all the time.

Until at last he looked over and beyond her shoulder . . . his glance searching the terrace, the pool. Oh, surely not looking for me! prayed Nicola in desperation. But it seemed he was. For now he was pointing her out to his companion, crooking a summoning finger to her—how *could* he?—and coming to the edge of the pool to wait for her.

She climbed out, thrusting back her wet hair with both hands, not daring to look at him. She felt sick and her heart was pounding high up in her throat. She sensed that Hans was close behind her, but effacing himself. Then Kurt's voice, urbane, cool, contained, was introducing her in French.

'This is Diane, Gesine.' And then, his eyes unwaveringly upon her face—'Madame Gesine Silber,

Diane. We met in Antibes, the summer I spent there, you may remember, before Father died? You two never met, did you? Indeed, you were still away at school at that time, I believe?'

Nicola took the warning. 'I was at Vevey, yes,' she agreed, glad that she need not lie, remembering that Diane had mentioned that Monsieur Thesige had not died until after she had left Vevey. She offered her hand and smiled, wondering if it were safe to give Madame Silber the courtesy of saying that Kurt had often spoken of her. If not, what could she say, with the ease he would expect of her if she were really Diane? For the moment she was saved by the other woman's own brilliant smile and her greeting.

'So you are Diane, Kurt's little sister? Not that you are anyone's "little sister" now!' She broke off with a deprecatory shake of her head. '*Chut*, my French! Would you mind if we spoke English instead? I am English, you see, and Kurt tells me yours is excellent. Which is why he brought you along to interpret for him with his clients.'

Nicola hid her surprise that such erotic gestures and looks had an English background. Somehow Gesine Silber had a completely cosmopolitan air. 'Gesine? Silber?' Neither name had an English sound, though the wedding-ring she wore could account for the 'Silber' at least. Nicola told her, 'Yes, I do speak English—better than Kurt does,' and went on in English, 'Are you on holiday in Lausanne, *madame*? From England? I daresay you and Kurt were very surprised to meet each other again if you hadn't met since he was in Antibes, which must be nearly five years ago now?'

'Just about all of that,' Gesine Silber agreed. 'But I was Gesine Belmont then, heavily chaperoned by my mother, on my first visit to the Riviera, and seeing it as my oyster for the opening.'

'You mean you *made* it your oyster. Against you, it never had a chance,' Kurt put in, his tone dry.

A throaty laugh and a shrug. 'You disapprove of me still—as you often did then—but who cared?' she mocked him.

'Who indeed? You rarely did, I noticed.'

'And so why should I? Isn't one only young once? And if not for snatching and taking all that they can offer, what are such playground places *for*? What's more, just because, that summer, you were a playboy in Antibes by no choice of your own, what right did that give you, my friend, to look down your long Swiss nose at a dedicated playgirl like me?' With another laugh which she probably intended to take the tartness out of that, Gesine turned back to Nicola and took the rest of her questions in turn.

'No, I'm not from England. From Beirut. Though I was born to a British passport, I've only touched the country in passing, as one says. I was born in India, of an English father and a Portuguese mother, and since I was a child there was almost everywhere for me *but* England. I am the widow of a businessman of even more mixed blood than mine—and no, I wasn't, in fact, surprised to meet Kurt in Lausanne. I knew he was to be here.'

'Oh——' At that Nicola looked at Kurt, who explained, 'Yes, Gesine, I find, is of our party. After Antibes we—lost touch, and I had no idea she had any connection with the Beirut firm of Silber and Silber, the horologists——'

'One Silber having been my husband; the other, Gregor, with whom I've come here, his cousin, and I, with more flair than expertise, whom Gregor encourages to dabble in engraving-design,' Gesine supplemented. 'And so here we are, staying at the Beau Rivage, Gregor agog for the latest in Swiss horology developments, and I, creeping up on Kurt unawares, agog for—now what *am* I agog for, would you suggest?' she challenged Kurt.

He looked at her through narrowed eyes, appraising her. 'As always—for the mystique and the acclaim you create for yourself without even trying, I'd say,' he told her, at which her deep laugh rang out again.

'Without *trying*? Ah, if he only knew the techniques we all employ—hm?' she enquired of Nicola, adding, 'And now I insist—you will both dine with Gregor and me tonight. I shall not take No.'

'On the contrary, you will,' said Kurt evenly. 'You will both dine with us. Say at eight-thirty? Diane, would you ring the villa for me and tell the Rallis we shall be four for dinner, please?'

Nicola hesitated, once more aware of Hans, still hovering in the background. 'For four? But I——' she began, then took refuge in introducing Hans to Gesine, before signalling Kurt aside, leaving them talking together.

'Hans Durer asked me to dinner this evening, and I accepted,' she whispered to Kurt.

'Then you must excuse yourself for tonight,' he said.

'How can I, when he heard you invite the Silbers

and will know that it is only to dine with them instead?'

Kurt said crisply, 'I'm sorry. It is not "only" to dine with them. It is to act as my hostess to Gesine and Gregor Silber, with whom I hope to do some very good business. Which, I'd remind you, is a part of your job. So run along now and phone Signora Ralli that we shall be four, and come back and beg Durer to excuse you for tonight.'

Nicola still lingered. 'I hate to let him down, when he knows what for——'

'Nonsense. As a businessman himself, he must understand business priorities. He'll excuse you all right.'

'I shall still hate asking him.'

Kurt exhaled a long breath from behind set teeth. 'And you are the cool *anglaise* whom I credited with having a shell as thick as a carapace! Still, I'll spare you embarrassment, if you like. While you are ringing the villa, I'll explain, man-to-man, to Durer how business matters stand, and invite him to dine with the rest of us instead. Will that do?'

Nicola sighed with relief. 'Oh would you, please?'

'Then make our numbers five to Maria Ralli,' Kurt said as he turned away.

Gregor Silber was a prosperous-looking man in his early forties with a thick white skin and an upbrush of greying hair. He spoke both French and English with accent, but was reasonably fluent in either language. At dinner English was spoken, as Hans Durer understood this best.

The table was round, making for intimacy. Kurt

52

had Gesine on his right, with Hans between her and Nicola who, opposite Kurt, had Gregor Silber on her right. None of the men talked business over the meal, and Nicola realised that this was the accepted etiquette of such affairs—they were merely the social backcloth for the hard contracts to be made later in other places.

Gesine, dressed for the evening, had a different but even more striking glamour than by day. Her blonde hair, with its broad silvery lock, was drawn up tautly from her face and swathed about by a high-piled and perfectly matched hairpiece. She wore gold jewellery with a brief gold lamé dress and allowed Kurt's hands to linger on her shoulders as he helped her to shrug out of its matching coat as they sat down to the meal.

Groomed and chic to the last curled eyelash, she had made a chameleon-change from her careless undress of the morning. And yet, thought Nicola, watching her, she had neither lost nor gained by the process. For, as Nicola thought they must surely know themselves, women like Gesine Silber had only to turn a head or flick a smile or crook a provocative eyebrow, for whatever scene they found themselves in to be theirs to play upon at will.

During the evening Nicola learned that Benno Silber, Gesine's late husband, had been senior to Gregor by five years; Benno had died suddenly; Gesine had been a wife for less than two years; Gregor was not married. Gesine, bored and idle after Benno's death, had shown some talent for design and now advised Gregor as well on trends in costume jewellery, which was the firm's sideline to its main wholesale trade in expensive clocks and watches.

Gesine airily dismissed her work as a mere hobby

53

she indulged to keep her out of mischief. But Gregor praised it extravagantly, making his praise part of his obvious homage to everything she was and did.

He is in love with her, was Nicola's intuitive thought. She knows it; she is pleased and flattered—but she does not care. She has time for him now and then, but probably only between other conquests, however casual—and tonight she has both Kurt and Hans, and could take several more hypnotised males in her stride . . .

Nicola glanced covertly at Kurt without catching his eye. She had not seen him to speak to since the morning, and she knew she must ask him how much she, as Diane, was supposed to know about his earlier acquaintanceship with Gesine.

Gesine had playfully let slip that he had 'dis-approved' of her at Antibes. Why had he? And what intimacy had they shared then which allowed her to remind him of it now, hinting that she had nothing to fear from it or from him—and, if Nicola read the signs aright, never had?

Gregor Silber—deep under Gesine's spell. Kurt too, perhaps, still? Though there were practical questions about the other woman which she must ask him for safety's sake, Nicola knew that 'Were you in love with her?' 'Are you?' was one she would not ask. Dared not . . . not wanting to know.

The meal moved smoothly towards its end, when Kurt suggested, 'If you'll take Gesine to the salon, Diane, we'll join you for coffee presently. Gesine?'

He was behind Gesine's chair, drawing it out for her. She rose and turned, but before moving away with Nicola, she looked her over, then back at Kurt.

'You know—so utterly unlike, you two!' she re-marked. 'Kurt so blond and you so dark—I declare, one could well suspect that one of you was a change-ling child, with a wicked nurse who sold her baby charge to the gipsies for gold! But which?'

At the cut, so lightly made, yet so near to the truth, Nicola caught her breath in sharp, unguarded alarm. She glanced at Kurt whose face hadn't moved a muscle.

He told Gesine gravely, 'Why, *I* was, of course! Didn't I ever tell you? That the old hag didn't only sell the real Kurt Thesige to the gipsies, but struck a pretty hard bargain for his cradle as well?' He turned to Nicola. 'Or that was how we always heard the story, wasn't it, Diane *ma mie*?' he said—and dropped a kiss upon her cheek.

She flushed, put her fingertips to the place his lips had touched, then managed a smile for the others.

'Yes, that was it,' she told them. 'Except that Kurt forgot the sequel—that she didn't get away with it, in the matter of the cradle, because the gipsies returned it later, claiming there was woodworm in the rockers, and asked for their money back.'

The moment of crisis passed in the general laughter which greeted that. Only for Nicola had it been a mo-ment of brief panic which Kurt had dispelled, and a moment of sensation, sweeter though no less disturb-ing, which she wished she hadn't experienced with anyone at all looking on.

That night before she slept she forced herself to face her growing awareness of Kurt as a man ... a man whose approval she wanted, whose criticism stung her, who was in her thoughts—too much.

She was nothing to him. In his rôle as her brother, he could kiss her in front of other people, mean nothing by it and remain completely oblivious of its effect on her—the surprise of it, the eager, warm pulse of her response to its coolness, her sense of its marking a before-and-after point of time for her. A 'before' of self-ownership and wholeness of heart; an 'after' of jealous wanting to love and be loved which was with her now, and would be as far as thought and hope and fear could look ahead.

But *love*! Was it possible to love so soon and so little encouraged? Physical attraction, yes. Infatuation, yes. She had known both in her time, had emerged unscathed, and would be glad to dismiss her feeling for Kurt as easily. But though she did her best to decry it with cold facts, she could not.

She knew so little of him. But for this brief crossing of their paths, he moved in an entirely different world. At a guess, he had lived for eight or ten more adult years than she had. He had a past which had known for a time the electric challenge of Gesine Silber; his present now knew it again. In between, though he had not married, there must have been other women in his life; he was a man of the world with plenty of opportunity. It was utter folly to love him. Yet it had happened, she knew.

And the solution? An escape route from an intolerable situation? There wasn't one, while she remained pledged to him until Diane was found. And what was he doing about that? When she had asked, he had snubbed her, and would be capable of doing so again. Besides, it was already too late for Diane to appear with Kurt in

Lausanne. For the term of his stay in the city, though no longer, the masquerade must be played out to the end he had planned for it.

The end . . . By no means for the first time, Nicola looked beyond it. If Diane had made no sign by then, finding her later was Kurt's and her family's affair. Back in their own cities and businesses, Kurt's clients would briefly remember their young hostess in Lausanne. But the hostess herself would never 'stop by' at any American home in answer to those kindly invitations. Kurt, presumably would have done the business he wanted. His temporary 'sister' would be paid off. No aftermath of scandal for him.

Unless—and the thought jerked Nicola unpleasantly from the very edge of long-sought sleep—*unless Gesine Silber did not go back to Beirut when her cousin went, but stayed.*

She claimed to have come purposefully, knowing she would meet Kurt again. Why? And if she lingered, what then for Kurt? For Diane? For Nicola? All of them caught in the web of their own making, as soon as just one other person learned the truth. Or could Kurt manipulate even *that*?

The next morning there was a heady, nervous excitement to meeting him. They both took their coffee and rolls in their own rooms and he was about to go out when Nicola came down.

'Can you spare me a few minutes?' she asked.

'Of course.' He came to rest a knee on the window seat, where she sat with her back to the light. He looked obliquely down at her. 'I'm to be taken to task for the form of my little compliment to you last night? You disapproved of me? Is that it?' he asked.

'You mean—your kissing me? I—didn't think it was necessary.'

'Pff! It was nothing, a *bagatelle*, all part of the act. When Diane was, say, thirteen or so, and I felt brotherly towards her, I'd probably have pulled her plaits. At the age she is now and I approved of her, I'd kiss her in just the way I kissed you. Except, I confess, that last night I was also inviting you to play along with the joke we were putting over—which you did, most gallantly.'

(For him—'all part of the act'. As if she didn't know!) She said a little shakily, 'It was just so unexpected, that's all.'

'And you needed your "few minutes" with me to rule, "Don't let it occur again, if you please," hm?'

'No. For something else.'

'Good. For I don't promise it might not occur again, if occasion arises. Such little tributes—*baisemains*, we call them—are the most natural thing in the world in our families; as commonplace as our habit of shaking hands, as you'd find if you married into one of them—— However, this other problem? What is it?'

'It's about Madame Silber—— That is, is she Madame or Mrs, or what?'

'I think she would prefer Madame. It has a suitable cosmopolitan flavour. But to you, as to me, she can be Gesine. And so what about her? You feel you ought to know as much as Diane would have heard about the Antibes scene, and whatever I have gathered myself of her present circumstances?'

'Please. For instance, I didn't understand what she meant about your being a playboy against your will——'

'—which, as Diane, you would have known, of course. Well, that referred to the idleness my father forced on me right up to the date he died.'

'Oh yes, I remember Diane told me——'

Kurt nodded. 'I was nearly thirty. I was convinced I had some flair for big business and I was alight with eagerness to show what I could do in *Thesige*. But because my methods would have been new ones and my father clung to the old, he kept me out as long as he could. So what was left to me? I drove, I skied, I gambled and idled with all the verve I'd have put into *Thesige* instead, if he had made any place for me—if only on the factory floor. And so—Monte Carlo, Davos, the Caribbean—they were all my playgrounds, and in Antibes that summer before my father's death, Gesine was there too.'

'On holiday?'

'A prolonged one—for a purpose. Her mother's purpose for her. Mrs Belmont was the Portuguese widow of an Englishman whose business in India had virtually collapsed. When he died, Mrs Belmont sold it for what she could get and on the capital set herself to achieving a rich, arranged marriage for Gesine before the money ran out. After all, I've allowed since that the woman wasn't to blame. In India she had seen marriages of convenience work well; to any Latin there is nothing shocking about them, and she had her own future to think of, as well as Gesine's.'

'And Madame Silber—Gesine—went along with this?'

Kurt's eyes fixed on the view from the window. 'That was the tantalising thing—she never allowed one to know,' he said. 'For a time I thought not, and also for a time Mrs Belmont let me suppose I was on her short list as a candidate.'

(Then he had been in love with Gesine!) Nicola's mouth felt dry. 'And weren't you?' she asked.

'Not after she realised that, though I had money enough for my bachelor state, I had no future prospects while my father lived. As she tactfully reminded me—"Rich fathers, my friend, have been known to make wills which disinherit sons they do not trust." And it was at about the same time that *I* realised Gesine's own thinking was on much the same lines. And so'—Kurt brought his glance back to Nicola— 'there you have more of the picture than Diane had at the time. My father died that autumn; I took command of *Thesige*, and until Gesine accosted me at La Harpe yesterday, I had heard no news of her since.'

And how little you have told me of what she meant ... means still to you, thought Nicola. Aloud she asked, 'Not even that she had married?'

'Not even that. Before I introduced you, she had sketched in the story for me. Her mother had died suddenly six months after Gesine had married Benno Silber, a hybrid middle European, who qualified as to both current wealth *and* prospects. Since his cousin died, Gregor has run the Silber business; she, of course, has financial interests in it; she came to Lausanne with Gregor, being "curious", she said, to meet me again.'

Kurt straightened and looked at his watch. 'Well, there you have it. Diane didn't know as much. Still, anything more you want to know, in order to feel at ease in Gesine's company?'

Nicola shook her head. 'No,' she lied, and let him go.

Later that morning the telephone rang three times.

The first time, it was Hans Durer on the line, making his bread-and-butter call of thanks for hospitality, and hoping that Nicola would keep their own dinner-date soon.

'I should like to,' she told him. 'It was good of you to oblige Kurt last night. I promise it shan't happen again.'

'Then this evening, perhaps? The same arrangement as before—I will call for you at the villa?'

They agreed on that and rang off. The second call was by Gesine, asking first for Kurt.

'I'm sorry, he is at the Palais this morning,' said Nicola.

'Tch! So is Gregor, and I'm bored. What are you doing yourself?'

'Er—nothing until a hair appointment at half past twelve, and this afternoon I am going to escort a party to Les Avants.'

'Les Avants? What is there?'

'Narcissi fields in full bloom. They are quite a sight.'

'The complete little courier, aren't you?' Gesine scoffed lightly. 'Am I invited to view narcissi fields too?'

'Of course—if you'd like to come.'

There was a sound as if Gesine yawned. 'Thanks, but I think not. Afternoons are a no-man's-land time of day, and I've lived long enough in the East to have the siesta habit ingrained. But I still need company. I shall ring Gregor at the Palais and tell him he is to bring Kurt back here for drinks before lunch without fail, and what about your coming for one yourself before your hair thing?'

Nicola looked at her watch, considering times. 'I should have to leave soon after noon,' she said.

'Well, that's all right. I'll expect you——'

The third call came just as Nicola was ready to leave the villa.

She picked up the receiver, spoke the villa's number and waited, to be greeted only by silence.

'Yes?' She gave the number again, adding, 'Diane Thesige speaking,' and that time thought she heard a sharply drawn breath at the other end of the line. Otherwise, still silence.

She tried once more, again without result except for a click which told of a replaced receiver, upon which she cradled her own, shaking a puzzled head as she did so.

When they rang, telephones ought to say something, even if it was only 'Sorry, wrong number' or 'Testing'! There was an unnerving, sinister quality to their silence if they did not. So who, wanting the villa, *hadn't* wanted it once they had got it, yet had hung on for a minute or two, not having the civility to say so? But to that question the now inert instrument offered no clue.

Kurt had the car, so she had decided to walk down to the Beau Rivage. But before she set out Signora Ralli waylaid her, wanting to discuss menus, so that it was some ten minutes later that she was waiting to cross the traffic-choked avenue towards the cool shade of the far pavements. By the nearest lamp-standard someone else was waiting too—a lean young man, hatless, bejeaned, shirtsleeves rolled up to his bronzed biceps—an artisan type. Looking his way, Nicola caught his eye and lifted her shoulder in a slight shrug of fellow-feeling over their shared delay. But he made no answering sign and when at last there was a gap in the traffic, he did not cross, but stayed where he was, motionless by the lamp-standard.

Waiting for his girl and giving me the brush-off for a forward hussy, thought Nicola, amused, and then promptly forgot him as she took the first branching avenue which led south to the Lake.

Gesine had left a message at the reception desk that Nicola was to go to her room, where she was up but dressed only in a negligée of pleated green silk. At her elbow was a tray of drinks, from which Nicola chose a dry sherry and sat down.

Gesine poured her own drink and offered cigarettes. 'Gregor has promised faithfully to bring Kurt down. Will you stay until they come?' she asked.

'I'm afraid I can't, unless they come very soon.'

'Which they won't. I could hardly pin Gregor at the telephone long enough to make him listen to me. *Men!* Once they are bitten by ambition, they're impossible. Tell me, when did this dedication to big business hit Kurt—you should know?'

Nicola hesitated. 'I don't know that it did "hit" him,' she said carefully. 'I think he always had it. It was Father who put the curb on him, you know.'

'Jealous of him or distrusting him?'

'I don't know. Only that Kurt was bitter about it, knowing what he could do.'

'And made little sister Diane his confidante, no

doubt?'

'He didn't have to. Ever since I've known Kurt—been aware of him as a person, I mean—I've realised just what a terrific driving-force his faith in himself is. A mountain has to be moved—and it moves, because he says so. It's—well, about as simple as that,' Nicola finished lamely, yet inwardly aware that she was neither lying nor embroidering; her love's awareness of Kurt knew it for the truth.

'Hm. Well, with all this dynamism in leash, it's a pity, isn't it, that he didn't allow it to spark to some purpose a bit earlier?' Gesine retorted thinly.

'What do you mean?'

'Why, surely? He could have forced his way into the firm, couldn't he? More or less taken it over?'

'He had too much respect for his father's—prejudices!'

'Even though showing some initiative and some decent prospects before it was too late would have enabled him to marry me?' A pause. 'Or perhaps you didn't know that, when we were together in Antibes, he wanted to—quite badly?'

Nicola said, 'I didn't know then. He has told me since.'

'When?'

'Some things—only yesterday, after I had met you.'

'The "some things" being to the effect that I had turned him down, I suppose. Well, he had only himself to blame, though I'd rather have expected that, in a fit of pique, he might have proposed later to the first appealing little chit who caught his eye. Why didn't he, do you know?'

'No. Perhaps you should feel flattered that he

didn't.'

'I'm much more intrigued as to what woman—or women—there are in his life now,' Gesine retorted. 'Now you must have some inkling about them?'

'I haven't. He doesn't confide in me.'

Gesine laughed. 'No? Still the "little sister" approach? I rather thought so, last night. But you shouldn't let him overdo it, you know. A too-hovering and too-protective brother is so apt to put other men off.'

'I don't know that I've ever found Kurt too solicitous of me,' said Nicola stiffly.

'Putting me in my place for suggesting you've any difficulty in either attracting men or keeping them, Kurt notwithstanding? My dear, nothing was further from my thoughts! Why, one had only to witness your young German at full eyework on you last night! But tell me, have you got Kurt's brotherly blessing for that affair?'

'I'm afraid I haven't asked his opinion of an affair that doesn't exist.'

Gesine pulled a wry face. 'Now you're offended, and I only meant a friendly warning. Because, as I read Kurt, he is quite equal to using his veto on an unsuitable match for you, if only as an answer to the thumbs-down he had from me.'

'Wouldn't that be very illogical of him?' Nicola asked as levelly as her rising temper allowed.

'Oh, my dear, as if any man's logic were ever a match for his wounded pride!'

Nicola ignored that. 'Not to mention,' she went on, 'that as I am of age and Kurt isn't my keeper, he'd have no right to interfere.'

'And yet I think you know he would, supposing you produced to him, say, a dustman, or even a pleasant nonentity like poor young Durer. After all, out of your own mouth, mountains move when Kurt says so——' Gesine broke off as Nicola put down her glass and stood. 'Oh dear, must you go already?'

'Yes. My hairdressing place is some way from here, and I'd like to walk.'

'*Walk?* Why, don't you drive a car?'

'Yes. But Kurt has ours, and he doesn't want me to drive in Lausanne.'

'And so you don't. I see.' Gesine's flat tone made that a statement which appeared to give her satisfaction, and Nicola left, feeling that rapiers had been drawn and used.

# CHAPTER FOUR

FROM her hair appointment Nicola returned to the villa by cab. After paying it off she was surprised to notice that, still by the same lamp-standard, stood the young man she had noticed earlier.

Exactly like a plain-clothes man in a police film, she thought idly as she turned towards the gate of the villa. But then the young man moved swiftly, lengthening his stride in order to meet her before she went through.

'Mademoiselle Thesige? Mademoiselle *Diane* Thesige?' he asked in French.

Nicola caught her breath. 'Yes,' she said.

'*No!*'

The sharp contradiction seemed to explode in her ears, and before she could challenge it, the young man went on urgently:

'You are not Diane Thesige, for that is impossible. I know she is not living here. But you could be Nicola Stirling, an English girl—am I right? No, *mademoiselle*, please——!'

He caught at her arm as she turned away, her panic utterly at a loss for a reply. 'Please, I beg of you, listen to me for a moment! I mean you no harm, but I know I must be right. You are this English girl, are you not?'

Nicola found her voice. 'And if I were not Mademoiselle Thesige, *monsieur*, what is that to you? I've never met you before. I certainly don't know who you are, nor why you think you have the right to question me.'

The young man held her glance compellingly. 'My name is Anton Pellerin. Ah, I see that you have heard it! Though not from Diane, I think? Then from whom?'

'From her brother, of course. From Kurt. So if you are Anton Pellerin, you'll have come from Diane. For you are the man who eloped with her, aren't you? And you know that she couldn't be here, because you know where she really is, and you are—together now?'

Distaste must have sounded in Nicola's tone, for Anton Pellerin frowned. 'We are *not* "together" in the way you meant that, *mademoiselle*. You make a slur upon Diane which I resent,' he said.

'I'd have thought you should realise you both invited such slurs when you persuaded her to leave with you as you did.'

'We had to take such opportunity as we could. We had no choice.'

'No choice?' Nicola echoed. 'No choice but to pick a method and a timing that could do nothing but harm to the reputation of *Thesige*? Leaving her brother in the lurch as Diane did was particularly cruel.'

Anton Pellerin insisted, 'No more cruel than his efforts to keep us apart. But you probably don't know much about that?'

'Something. Enough, perhaps. Kurt Thesige believed he had reason.' Nicola looked at her watch, seeing to her dismay that she had less than a quarter of an hour before collecting her party for Les Avants. She said, 'I'm sorry, I have to go. But why did you come and wait all this while to waylay me? What do you want? And at least you will tell me where Diane is now?'

'Not without your promise that you will not pass her whereabouts to her brother, and not untill you and I have had some more talk together, *mademoiselle*.'

Nicola shook her head. 'I'm not giving that promise. Kurt Thesige has a right to know, and your not telling me only makes me suspect that all he said of you may be true. And now, please, I have to go——'

Anton Pellerin agreed sullenly, 'And one can guess *what* Kurt Thesige had to say of me—though none of it true.' He laid a hand again on her arm. 'So please! Even if I don't keep you now, there are things I need to hear from you; things you must hear from me. For Diane's sake ... for Diane's good. So will you meet me again—wherever you like to say? This evening some time?'

'I can't tonight, and I shall be out all the afternoon too.' Nicola added, 'You may have guessed that I am doing my best to help Kurt in things Diane should have done for him. So I'd have to make it tomorrow.'

'Tomorrow morning, then. And where? Do you know a little café-bar, Pierre, on the Rue Liseron, near the Lausanne-Ouchy station?'

'Down near the front? No, but I'll find it. I know the Beau Rivage Hotel, of course, which isn't far from Liseron, is it?'

'No, a mere stone's throw. At eleven o'clock—will you be there?'

'Yes.' Nicola turned in at the gateway of the villa,

asking herself for a second despairing time—what had she done?

That evening Hans arrived for her while she was still dressing, and when she went down Kurt was giving him a drink.

'Where are you taking Diane?' Kurt asked.

'I don't know.' Hans looked at Nicola. 'Wherever she would like to go. When I asked her for last night, I suggested Vevey. But she shall choose.'

Nicola said, 'I'd like Vevey. I haven't been for a long time.' She turned to Kurt. 'Will you be in when we get back?'

'I don't know. I have some work to do, but I might adjourn somewhere for an after-dinner drink. You won't be too late?'

Hans smiled. 'I'll take good care of her, Monsieur Thesige.'

'Do. She's quite—valuable.' Putting a careless arm across Nicola's shoulder as they went out into the hall, Kurt asked Hans, 'By the way, I'm taking a party across the Lake to the Casino at Evian tomorrow evening. Would you care to join us, my friend?'

'I'd like to very much.'

'Good. We shall be meeting here and I've hired a launch. Don't bother to come by car though. We can give you a lift to the Quay.'

As he drove fast along the lakeshore road Hans asked, 'I wonder if you know why I'd like to see Vevey in particular? Can you guess?'

Nicola said, 'No. It's a picturesque place, but there is nothing very special about it. There's not much night life; further afield, it is best known for its schools.'

'Ah well, there you have the clue.' Hans turned his pleasant smile on her. 'You were at school there, weren't you? And I should like to see where.'

'I can't think why!'

'Because then I shall be able to imagine you there—just one of the several things I'd like to know about you. So you will show me where?'

'Of course, if you want to see.'

'Well, don't you, if you haven't been back for some time? Would you even like to go in—pay it a visit?'

'Oh no!'

He glanced at her again, frowning now. 'Why, weren't you happy there—Diane?'

'Yes, very happy. But do you think it's wise ever to go back?'

'No, perhaps not. But I'd still like to see a place where you spent some of the years when I didn't know you,' said Hans, accepting her false excuse for not making herself known again in a place where she had been Nicola Stirling, not Diane Thesige.

A few kilometres outside Lausanne they took the Corniche road through the vineyards of the Lavaux region, rejoining the main road just before Vevey. Nicola directed Hans to one of the older avenues of the town and showed him, apparently to his satisfaction, the austere mansion standing in its own grounds where Diane had been at school and where she herself had spent two happy years.

Over dinner at a pleasant restaurant overlooking the lake she made Hans laugh with her story of how Bertrand, the school Head's huge Alsatian, always patrolled so far ahead of his mistress that his appearance

71

at any of the popular cafés allowed any truants, out in search of chocolate cakes or ice creams, to make good their escape back to school before Madame caught them up. And afterwards, as a young moon had risen, Hans suggested they drive on through Montreux and look at the island castle of Chillon by moonlight.

It was an undemanding, restful evening, and Hans an easy companion. She had never met a man who talked less about himself; his curiosity was all for her. Once or twice, glancing furtively at his profile as he drove, she found she was thinking, *What a very nice person you are*, wondering what he would think about her deception if he knew of it, yet somehow able to feel that his judgment of her would be less harsh than the world's.

In his company she would—almost—forget the coil in which she was involved. Tomorrow she had to face her rendezvous with Anton Pellerin, but tonight, between that threat and between Kurt's cold calculation of her 'value' to him, there was the contrast of Hans, his interest in her spurred only by his liking for her, with no selfish overtones at all. And when, later, parting from her at the villa and refusing to go in with her, he hesitated for a moment and then only put his lips to her hand, she was grateful to him for asking no more of her than her conscience could justify to Kurt's warning against getting involved.

Pierre's Bar boasted a tiny apron of outside terrace and within was as dark as a cavern behind its gay sun-awnings. A snack counter ran its length from front to back and Nicola, early at the rendezvous, chose a table deep in its interior at which to wait for Anton Pellerin.

He was punctual. Nicola asked for a *café-au-lait*; he ordered a cognac for himself. As he sat down he said, 'Like you yesterday, I am rather pressed for time. I had twenty-four hours' leave from my foreman, but I shall have outstayed that by the time I get back today.'

'Back to where, and to what work?'

'A garage in Montreux. I am a qualified driving instructor and also a skilled motor mechanic, *mademoiselle*.'

'Yes, I know. And is Diane in Montreux too?' Nicola asked.

He looked her straight in the eye. 'I am trusting you. Yes, Diane is there too.'

'But you are not together, you say?'

'No, we are both working. I have lodgings, and she is living at a guest-house where she is the receptionist. We are usually able to see each other for a little while every day.'

'But *why*?'

He seemed to understand all that the question asked. 'We saw our escape as the only way to prove to Kurt Thesige that we were serious about marriage. He has the power to veto it for Diane, as perhaps you know, and also just how he regards my courtship of her?'

'I think so. He sees you as a fortune-hunter.'

A nod. 'Exactly—and Diane as being as moonstruck as she was once for a worthless man. Which I am not, nor a money-seeker either. So Kurt Thesige is rich, of long, proud family and a craftsman? Well, I was born to no silver spoon. My father is a baker in Zürich and my mother was a hospital nurse. But there's as much precision to my trade as to Kurt's; a skilled man in my job doesn't need to go cap in hand for good pay, and there is nothing I would not ask these hands to do for Diane'—bronzed and capable, they were spread for Nicola's inspection—'*nothing!*'

Nicola sighed, as much for her own bewilderment as for a sincerity which for some reason hadn't got through to Kurt. She asked next, 'But what did you hope to gain by running away? What *have* you gained so far?'

Anton thought for a moment. Then, 'Time, mainly,' he said. 'Time to show Kurt that we are willing to wait to marry, if necessary. To wait *innocently* —you know what I mean?'

'Yes.'

'I am glad. We have also gained time to see as much of each other as was not permitted to us in Neuchâtel without unhappiness for Diane. And for both we need still more time yet—which is why I wanted your promise that Kurt should not learn where we are.'

'They why did you show up yesterday, watching the villa, watching for me? Kurt might have seen you. What then?'

'I saw him go out, and I made sure that he didn't. Then I telephoned the villa from a booth in the Avenue.'

'That was *you*? And I told you——'

'That you were Diane Thesige, yes. Which was something deeper than I could understand. I do not understand it still. But I came, *mademoiselle*——'

Nicola interrupted, 'Nicola, please. I'm Diane's friend, you know.'

'Thank you. I know it, and so does Diane, which was why she felt she could ask you to take the edge of

Kurt's anger on her behalf. Afterwards she was sorry, and she has suffered such remorse since at the way she left him that I took it upon myself to come to find out how he was placed and who, if anyone, had taken over the duties she should be doing for him here. She rather hoped that it might be you.'

'Why should she think so?' asked Nicola sharply.

'Well, if you had stayed in the flat as she asked you, you would have met Kurt. If so, he would have had to explain matters to you, and as you were free and meant to stay in Lausanne for a time, and could do it, she was sure, she thought Kurt might just offer you a job to play hostess for him. But she didn't expect——' Anton broke off, looking embarrassed.

Nicola supplied—'To find me installed in the villa and answering to her name, I daresay?'

'No.'

'Then she evidently hasn't grasped the size of the scandal she invited for Kurt by leaving him as she did. He did offer me the job, but as he explained, once it was known he had had to find a substitute hostess, it would not be long before the news of Diane's defection would be out. The newshounds would be on to it; her aunt might hear of it or have to be told. And so——' Briefly and baldly, sparing him none of the details, Nicola related Kurt's solution of the crisis to Anton.

When she had finished he looked at her with puzzled admiration, as he said, 'This took a great deal of courage, and you did it for Diane? So now I can tell her that I've seen you and that, thanks to you, the worst hasn't happened for Kurt?'

'She should thank Kurt himself more, and if she

75

has any feeling at all for his difficulties, she could let him know now where she is,' Nicola advised.

Anton shook his head. 'She will not do that yet, and if you remember, I asked your promise that you would not tell him either.'

'Now shall I. But Diane should!'

'No. For though I think I have convinced you of our good faith, Kurt Thesige isn't to be persuaded so easily. Time only, we believe, will do it, and therefore time we must have. Try to see that ... Nicola ... please?'

She ignored the appeal. For Kurt's sake, she had to. 'But how *much* time? Weeks? Months? *How* long?' she demanded wildly.

Anton shrugged. 'I don't know, but more than we have had yet. And meanwhile, I have your word?'

She stood up. 'Unwillingly—but yes,' she told him, and then, 'I'll leave alone, if you don't mind?'

He nodded agreement, letting her go. But as she reached the door, standing aside to allow some people —three men and a woman—to come in, he was calling her name and plunging after her.

'Nicola! Your scarf!'

'Oh, thank you.' She turned and took from him the silk headsquare which she had pulled off and which must have slipped from her lap at the table. By this time the four people were taking stools at the long counter, and she glanced across at them.

Two of the men were strangers, but the third was Gregor Silber and the woman, glancing back over her shoulder, as if aware of Nicola's eye upon her, was— Gesine.

For Nicola the moment seemed frozen in time.

Then Gesine looked away without a flicker of recognition. *But what had she heard?*

For the rest of the day Nicola's thoughts were in a turmoil; of dismay at the turn events had taken; of reasoning for and against breaking her promise and telling Kurt where Diane was, and fear that Gesine had not only heard Anton call her by name, but had recognised her too.

That she had heard Anton's call of 'Nicola!,' there was not much doubt. The whole café must have heard it. She must also have seen that a girl had turned, thanked him and had taken the scarf from him. But had she known Nicola for that girl? Or could Nicola hope that, as Gesine had made no sign, her eyes had been momentarily as bemused as her own had been, on coming in from the sunshine outside?

Whether or not was something only Gesine knew. Unless she questioned the incident the next time they met, Nicola never would. Even if Gesine said nothing, she would never be sure ... never feel safe. And meanwhile she suffered all the fruitless hindsight there was.

Why on earth had she let Anton choose for their meeting place a bar almost within shouting distance of the Silbers' luxury hotel? And what crass lack of caution on her part had made him free of 'Nicola' as her name, when she should have warned him that here she must be 'Diane' to him as to everyone else? Two hideous mistakes in a matter of twenty-four hours! How many more might she expect to make before she had to go to Kurt to confess failure, with all the scandal of exposure that would mean for him, for them both, for Diane?

She was not to be left long in doubt that Gesine had recognised her, though at least Gesine did not hint as much until they were alone together.

That evening Gesine and Gregor Silber were the first to arrive for the trip to Evian, coming on from another party they had attended earlier. Kurt offered drinks which Gregor accepted, but Gesine appealed to Nicola—'I wonder, could I freshen up a little first? Gregor was fussing that we should be late to you, and he wouldn't let me go back to the hotel before we came on. Do you mind?'

'Of course not. I'll take you to my room.' Nicola led the way upstairs, showed Gesine to her bedroom and her bathroom and was about to leave her when Gesine said :

'What's your hurry? Gregor made us too early, as usual. I often tell him he will turn up half an hour too soon for his own funeral. So wait, won't you, and talk to me while I put on my face?'

'If you want me to.' Nicola waited until she came through from the bathroom and, seating herself at Nicola's dressing-table, began work on her make-up from the assortment of miniature bottles and *coffrets* which she produced from a handbag beauty-case. She used moisturising cream, sprayed toning lotion, patted in foundation, concentrating in a dedicated silence until, smoothing and blending eyeshadow, she addressed Nicola's reflection in the mirror, smiling faintly, her tone arch.

'You know, I was *so* intrigued by that little scene this morning! At Pierre's Bar, where Gregor and I had been lured by these two types we had met in the hotel, who claimed that Pierre's *fondue* was out of this world for flavour. It wasn't. I've tasted far better. But do tell me, were you on the track of the perfect *fondue* too? Or had that handsome young pick-up made a date to meet you there?'

Nicola felt her colour drain from her face. 'I——— He hadn't———'

Gesine turned on the dressing-stool. 'My dear! I'm not going to tell on you to Kurt—what do you think? I mean, if he disapproves of the boy Durer lifting his eyes to you, you could hardly expect his enthusiasm for this other conquest either, could we? Er—virile, earthy, but *not* quite up to the present Thesige standard, would you say? So naturally my lips will stay sealed. Not a word shall Kurt hear from me. Though to think'—facing again to the mirror and going on with her work, Gesine laughed shortly, as if at her own folly—'to think that I believed you couldn't say No to brother Kurt, and yet when you wanted to indulge in a clandestine affair, you even had the wit to use an alias! Now what was it? Nicole...? No, Nicola, I think—yes? And not very pleased either that you had been seen?'

Nicola thought swiftly, realising she must let pass this mistaken reading of the scene Gesine had witnessed. She said, 'I didn't know you had recognised me. That's why I didn't stay. But I'm not having an affair with that young man. I was having a coffee at Pierre, and he joined me at my table. We got into conversation and———'

'And he asked you your name, and you, crafty child, gave him a false one, just in case he might make himself a nuisance? Well, well, I couldn't have done much quicker thinking myself! And if you want to see him again, don't mind me. I'm no telltale, and Kurt shan't know.' Dusting powder lightly, smoothing her brows with a fingertip, Gesine wiped her hands on a handkerchief which she flicked from her bag then frowned at the soiled smudge on the linen.

'Tch, look at that! And I haven't a spare. My dear, I wonder? Would you mind——?'

Nicola opened a drawer. 'Of course not. Help yourself.'

'Very sweet of you.' Gesine selected a handkerchief, shook it out and indicated that she was ready to go down. When they rejoined the men in the salon, most of Kurt's other guests had arrived, and when the muster was complete, they adjourned to the available cars and drove down to the Quay.

The surface of the lake was like black silk; the moon not yet risen. For Nicola the short journey across to the French shore was all too short; worried and heart-sick, she would have liked to prolong it far beyond the point of time when she must talk brightly again to near-strangers; be good company; match their gaiety with her own; be . . . Diane.

The Casino was typical of its kind, its doors open to throngs of diners, dancers, drinkers, card-playing devotees, hard-faced habitués of the tables—a cosmopolitan crowd of pleasure-seekers gathered for one night into a common mass which, tomorrow, would break into a thousand pieces when the people who had composed it went their separate ways.

Nicola danced—with Hans, sedately with Gregor Silber, once with Kurt, and with two of the American men. Kurt's party dined at a single long table, Kurt as host at its head, Nicola as hostess at its foot, a whole table-length away from Gesine on Kurt's right; Gesine, gauntly elegant and vivacious and, in a mainly male company, as assured of an audience as always.

Their guests drank to the success of Kurt's sales convention; Kurt, to Nicola's embarrassment, toasted 'our hostess, Diane'. Random flashlight pictures were taken and offered round later. Nicola was relieved to see that in the one or two in which she figured she might have been almost anyone. The same freelance photographer also had caught one of Gesine with Kurt, and of Kurt alone. Of the latter Nicola asked the man, 'How much?'

'Three francs, *mademoiselle*.'

'I'd like it.' She paid for it and put it in her bag— the only photograph of Kurt she was ever likely to have. Later he came in search of her; took her by the hand. 'I'm going to stake you to a session at the tables,' he said. 'Gregor Silber is doing the same for Gesine, and we'll see if we can top their winnings.'

In fact, after a short spell of luck for each of them, they both struck a long sequence when they had to watch their stakes disappear under the croupier's relentless rake. Finally Gesine emerged a few francs to the good; Nicola made a loss. As Gregor drew out Gesine's chair at Kurt's suggestion they should go to the bar for a drink before leaving, she shrugged. 'Ah well, perhaps we are both luckier at other things than at gambling. In England they say, "Unlucky at cards; lucky in love," did you know?' she asked Nicola.

'Yes, I'd heard it.' Nicola was watching Kurt who had stooped at Gesine's feet. He stood up, a handkerchief in his fingers. 'You dropped this,' he began to

Gesine, and then withdrew it. 'Or no, it's not yours. The initials——' and he showed her the embroidered 'N.S.' in its corner.

'But it is mine,' Gesine claimed. 'That is, it is Diane's really. She lent it to me, the good child.'

'*Diane's?*' Kurt's echo was blank; the swift look he threw at Nicola, an annoyed question she understood only too well. He handed over the handkerchief to Gesine. 'How was one to know? Diane should check her returning laundry better, shouldn't she?' he said, his tone dismissing the incident as far as Gesine was concerned.

Gesine agreed, 'She should indeed. Careless of her—— Unless of course'—the glance she shared between them was full of bright mischief—'unless she is leading a double life of which you know nothing, my friend! Say a *demi-monde* role that calls for an alias. "N." Now what, in the half-world of intrigue, could "N" stand for? "Ninon", perhaps? "Nana?" As for the "S", how could one arrive at that without working right through the "S" pages of the telephone directory?'

'As you say—impossible. Much more likely, I think, that Diane has somehow managed to win herself a handkerchief to which she has no right. Shall we go?' Kurt asked, moving off with Gregor Silber, though leaving Nicola under no illusion that she had heard the last of her carelessness from him.

But for the rest of the evening they were not alone together. Hans claimed her for another dance and after that the party gathered itself by twos and threes for the return to Lausanne.

The night was much colder now and when the launch had put out from the quay a sharp breeze coming off the lake sent most people to the shelter of the aft saloon. But not everyone. Kurt was not there, nor was Gesine, nor Gregor Silber. Nicola went there with Hans, but presently finding the air too warm, too thick with cigar and cigarette smoke, she 'lost' Hans on purpose and slipped out on deck.

She walked over to the nearest lee rail and leaned on it, watching the dark slick of the water. On the same rail, both aft and forward of her, there were other figures; talk; laughter. But tired of company, worried over her handkerchief *gaffe*, she did not want to join any of them, and so went over to the windward side. There she was alone, and the wind was keen. She pulled up the deep shawl collar of her coat and held it close against her ears, resting her elbows on the rail. So, the cloth and her cupped hands making her deaf, she did not hear Gregor Silber approach until he spoke to her.

'You have chosen a chilly spot, *mademoiselle*. Did you want to be alone?'

She let her collar fall. 'No, I came out because it was rather airless in the saloon. Did you find it so too?'

'I didn't try it. I guessed it would be, quite soon.' He lit a cigarette with difficulty against the wind. 'In fact, I'm in search of Gesine. I've done the round of the deck several times, and there is no sign of her, nor of your brother. Do you suppose they didn't join the launch for some reason?'

Nicola said, 'Oh no, I didn't see Kurt come aboard, but if he had meant to stay behind, I'm sure he would have told me. So he—and your cousin must be somewhere. They could have gone into the saloon while you've been on deck, or—there are several couples on the lee side on the rails, you know.'

'Each of whom I have disturbed in turn and been none too popular in consequence,' Gregor said humourlessly. 'No, it's a mystery, on so small a craft. They *must* have stayed behind.'

'I don't believe it.' Nicola knew she didn't want to. She levered herself from the rail and turned. 'Let's go round the deck again. Anyway, we shall be in to Lausanne in a few more minutes, and Gesine will have to show up then.'

'If she is on board.' Gregor fell into step and they turned aft first, then along the lee side, forward towards the half-covered sundeck and the heavily curtained wheelhouse beyond.

They halted in the shadow of the overhang to the sundeck, where there was no one. But up on the half-deck immediately behind the wheelhouse there was movement. Someone was there—two people; Gesine and Kurt. Close . . . locked in embrace. Gesine, her back to the watchers, unaware; Kurt, raising his head, seeing them, Nicola was certain, and then, keeping Gesine turned from them, letting his hand drop to her waist and moving with her to the rail.

Gregor drew a long, strangled breath. 'So——' he said, more to himself than to Nicola, and turned away.

Nicola turned with him. Glancing at his stricken face, she knew it was a mask for a pain which matched her own. 'I'm—sorry,' was all she could find to say.

He looked down at her. 'Don't be. Or rather, don't distress yourself for me. I have seen it coming. That's why Gesine wanted to come with me to Lausanne—to meet Kurt again. I should have known. Did *you* know he was still in love with her? That he wanted her still?'

'He has only told me that he wanted to marry her once, and that she turned him down, and later married your cousin.'

'And now she is a widow and he is a rich, successful man. Nothing between them now,' said Gregor, not guessing that he spoke a knell for Nicola too.

The launch juddered, lost speed, edged in to the quay and was made fast. The gangplanks went down; people gathered on the quay, calling their thanks and goodnights before adjourning to their cars. Nicola was glad that Gregor had the dignity to refuse Kurt's invitation to him and Gesine to go back to the villa. They offered Hans a lift to his hotel. Kurt and Nicola were the last to leave the quay.

In the car, 'Tired?' Kurt asked.

'A little.'

'But on the whole, a successful evening, wouldn't you say?'

'I'm glad.' A pause. 'I'm sorry about that handkerchief,' Nicola added.

'Mm—an awkward moment. How did it happen?'

'I don't know. I thought I'd sorted out every one of my initialled things, but I must have missed that. I'll go through everything again to make sure.'

'Yes, do that. And please be more careful in future.'

At the villa Signora Ralli, who had expected they would bring some guests back with them, was still up and had drinks and percolating coffee awaiting them. Kurt thanked her and dismissed her, and asked Nicola not to go when she was about to say goodnight.

'A nightcap?' He indicated the drinks' tray.

'No, thanks, I've had enough.'

'So have I, probably.' He considered the bottles for a moment, then pushed the tray aside. 'I suppose I should have warned you about that scene you happened to witness tonight?' he said.

'There was no reason why you should. You mean you knew it was going to happen?' Nicola asked.

He met her eyes frankly. 'I intended it should—some time. Though of course I couldn't have foretold the exact timing, nor that you and Gregor Silber would be there when it did.'

'He was worried as to where Gesine was, and we had been looking round the launch for her without finding either her or you.'

'She wanted to see the wheelhouse and I begged the privilege for her. We were probably there when you were looking.'

'Yes. Gregor Silber—minded, I think. He is in love with Gesine. Does she know?'

'Aren't women always supposed to "know"?' Kurt parried. 'But she doesn't love him, so he has nothing to lose in the long run.'

'He thinks he has. But as he says, she is a widow now and free, and he admits he knows she came here out of curiosity to see you again.'

'And since she did, the curiosity not all on her side. Or do you consider, since she had turned me down once, I should have more pride than to say so?'

'No. I suppose it was to be expected.'

'You understand that? You have known it yourself? You have finished with a man; he has done with you. Then you meet again and a question stirs—"What was there for me in him? What for him in me? Is it there still?" It has sometimes happened for you like that?'

Nicola shook her head. 'I can see that it could. But for me it never has.'

Kurt laughed shortly. 'Of course, I forgot. You have this tidy, disciplined heart that scorns to look back, and denies its scars. But we're not all so coolly endowed, I'm afraid. I, for one, needed to know how far my own scars had healed—if they had, and what current promise there was—if any.'

'And tonight you decided to find out?'

'Tonight I began to find out.'

For Nicola the small silence she made no attempt to break had the quality of an airlock; on the one side the question he would naturally expect her interest to put next; on the other her inability to ask it, fearing the answer too much. And when, after a moment she had said nothing, Kurt turned again to the tray of drinks.

'Perhaps I need one after all,' he said. 'May I tempt you? No? Then goodnight.'

'Goodnight.' She turned away, regretting the airlock too late. For if she had asked him what he had found out about himself and Gesine, he would have told her. And knowing was often easier to bear than fearing . . . wasn't it?

# CHAPTER FIVE

A DAY or two later Nicola was to learn—though not from Kurt himself—the steps he was taking to trace Diane; the occasion being a sequel to the arrival of a letter addressed to "Mlle Diane Thesige" in a handwriting she did not know. By the same post there was another letter for Diane, its postmark Paris, which she handed unopened to Kurt, sorting through his own correspondence.

He looked at the envelope and nodded. 'Yes, from Aunt Agathe. I'll deal with it—make some excuse for Diane's not writing herself. What is the other one? Shall I cope with that too?'

But Nicola had already seen its postmark, Montreux, and she was warned. 'No, this is only something local,' she said.

'For Diane, though?'

'No, from a shop—for me.'

'A bill? Shall I take care of it?'

'No, not a bill. Just'—she found a half-truth to tell him—'I had a string of pearl beads rethreaded, and it's ready for me to collect.' As she spoke she had opened the letter, made a show of reading it and put it in her bag.

'Right.' Kurt made a pile of his letters and stood. 'Did I tell you I'm taking a party back to Neuchâtel tomorrow? We shall tour the works and there's to be a day's session of lectures at the Institute of Horology.

We shall be away for three nights in all. I shan't take the car.'

Nicola said, 'Yes, you did tell me. Just the men, I suppose? The women won't be going too?'

'Oddly enough, most of them have chosen to go along. I'll let you know later those who are staying behind. Gesine, for one. So see something of her, will you, while we're away? She has never been very good company for herself.'

*And the very last company I'd choose,* was Nicola's unspoken thought. And yet a twinge of candour at the back of her mind knew that was not wholly the truth, that in being with Gesine she found a kind of cruel fascination; a magnetism of the chosen for the rejected which her pride despised but which her will only half wanted to resist. (Kurt had loved Gesine once, and if he wanted her still, what was the particular magic she worked for him? The empty, futile questions with which jealousy nagged at the heart!, As if it were possible to know!)

As soon as she was alone she opened Anton Pellerin's letter. It was very short.

'I daren't risk another telephone call, but I must see you. I can only spare a morning this time, so please— the same place as before; Tuesday. I shall wait until noon.'

Nicola tore the paper into shreds. No one should have the chance to read a romantic assignation into *that*! Tuesday was today. Lightning was supposed not to strike twice, so Pierre's Bar was probably as safe a rendezvous as any. And she had no commitments of her own until the late afternoon.

This time Anton was before her and as soon as she

joined him he thrust a Swiss newspaper in front of her. His forefinger stabbed at an item in the Personal column. 'Read that,' he said.

Nicola did so. It carried his name in larger type and said, 'If you are interested in the cash value of your proposition, state your figure and it will be met. Address yourself to K.T.' There followed a box number, care of the journal.

'You understand?' Anton demanded angrily. 'Kurt Thesige is trying to *buy* me off! He actually believes he can!'

Nicola looked up. 'But he can't?'

Anton exploded. 'You dare to ask that! You *ask* it! What do you think?'

'I'm sorry, I had to know. Does Diane know Kurt has done this?'

'Of course. And she is of the same mind as I am—that he should think again, and meanwhile keep his insulting cash offers to himself.' Anton added, 'A question she wanted me to ask you too—did you know he meant to do this?'

'No. When I asked him how he meant to try to trace Diane, he refused to discuss it with me, and I haven't mentioned her since. But however insultingly you and she see this move, wouldn't you be wise to answer it?' Nicola urged.

'And listen to the kind of conditions the man would impose? First of all, an address for Diane, where he could find her and go to work on her; then an under-taking from me that I wouldn't see her again, and then the buying-off price he would pay. You can't be serious,' scorned Anton.

'I am. After all, you don't have to agree to anything

Kurt demands, and sooner or later you and Diane will have to come out into the open and make him see you don't mean to be parted. You've got to convince him that you aren't to be bought off—if you aren't. And you've managed to convince me of that.'

'Which is not enough. You are not a purse-and-family-proud Thesige,' Anton pointed out. 'No, it's going to be later rather than sooner that we approach Kurt for terms, and when we do it will be by our choice, not his.'

'Even though you can't marry without his consent?'

'Even though. We can wait to marry, if we must.'

Nicola sighed for an obstinacy which matched Kurt's in its way, with herself and Diane the pawns in this battle of male wills. She made a last effort. 'Look,' she begged, 'will you tell me Diane's address and let me talk to her? Don't you think you both owe me that at least?'

Anton hesitated. 'Her address? How do I know you are to be trusted with it?'

'You trusted me with "Montreux" for you both, and if I had passed that on to Kurt, do you suppose he couldn't have found ways of tracing you there?' Nicola countered.

'True. You mean that if I gave you the address, you would go over and see Diane there?'

'If she would see me, and I hope you'll persuade her. Tomorrow or the next day. Kurt is going to Neuchâtel with a party and I shall be more or less free.'

'Very well.' Anton wrote the address of the *pension* where Diane was working, and handed it over. 'But I warn you, Diane thinks as I do, and persuasion otherwise from you won't do any good.'

'I'll risk it. It seems to me that it can't do much *less* good than any of us are achieving now,' was Nicola's crisp retort.

When he had left her she decided to go to Montreux the next day. But how? Though Kurt would have left the car for her use, she had his veto against driving it. No one must know of her errand, which meant she must not enlist Signor Ralli as her chauffeur. She would have to go by bus. It was the least conspicuous way.

However, an unwelcome alternative was to be thrust on her. The bus terminus was not far from the Beau Rivage Hotel, and as she was waiting in the appropriate queue, Gesine came past.

At sight of Nicola she halted. 'What on earth are you doing?' she demanded.

As the bus labelled 'Montreux' was just drawing alongside, it was futile to lie. 'I'm going over to Montreux, to see a school-friend who is working there,' Nicola told her.

'By why by bus? Why not go by car? Oh, of course —no big brother available, and he doesn't let you drive it here? Still, come out of that silly queue, do,' Gesine urged. 'Bus indeed! Or has Kurt taken your car?'

'No, he left it behind.'

'Then what are we waiting for? Like you, I'm left to twiddle my thumbs with boredom. So we'll take a taxi back to your villa, collect the car and I'll drive you to Montreux—why not?'

(Why *not*!) Nicola drew a sharp breath. 'Oh, I couldn't trouble you.'

'Nonsense, it would be a charity. I've got my own driving licence with me and the car has its papers, I suppose? Nothing more simple, surely?'

Nicola realised there was nothing for it. Her continued refusal would arouse more suspicion than she could afford. Gesine had accepted her motive for the trip and she would just have to rely on the good chance that Gesine might not mention her errand to Kurt.

They collected the car. Preparatory to moving off Gesine assured Nicola, 'You needn't look so harassed. I shan't spill you on the road. Driving a car happens to be one of the accomplishments I've perfected over the years. I have others—— Now, which way do we go?'

Nicola told her and left her to concentrate on the traffic. There was silence for quite a while until, with a glance along her shoulder, Gesine went on lightly:

'You rather missed your cue, my dear. I'm disappointed. I was hoping you might show some curiosity as to what my other accomplishments are.'

'If I had asked, would you have told me?' Nicola asked carefully.

Gesine laughed. 'Should I have mentioned them if I hadn't wanted to boast of them? For one—I'm beating age to a standstill, I hope. For, believe it or not, I've turned thirty. How old are you? Kurt did tell me.'

'I'm twenty'—Nicola despised the need to lie—'twenty-two.'

'Are you sure? You sound doubtful—or as if you were at an age where you had to keep it a dark secret,' Gesine taunted. 'However, since you ask—or didn't you?—I'm also quite pleased with the way I've

93

learned to manage men.'

'And do you really want to "manage" them?'

'Don't sound so shocked! Most of them need managing, as you'll discover. You'll tell them just as much as you think they should know; they'll enjoy having to guess the rest, and you will enjoy making them. I learned the art with my husband Benno, and Gregor answers to the same treatment, I find. Others too. Kurt——'

'You knew Kurt before you knew either your husband or Gregor,' Nicola reminded her. 'Could you manage him too?'

Gesine compressed her lips and looked straight ahead. 'I was younger then. Too much under my mother's thumb. I let Kurt go when I needn't have done, if I had the will I have now. And now Kurt is in a class by himself. If I still want him, I may have to watch my step. Since Antibes he has learnt a good deal too much about women for my liking, and I'd give a lot to know how and when and with whom.'

'And do you still want him?' Nicola asked.

Gesine sent her another slanted look. 'If I want to marry again, and the present alternatives being Gregor and Kurt, which would *you* choose? Oh, I forgot——!' She broke off. 'As if a sister would know! Even about a changeling brother which Kurt claimed he was. Do you remember—that night when I teased you both about your being so unlike?'

'Yes.'

'And you blushed to the roots of your hair, hating the "big brother" way he kissed you!'

'I didn't!'

'Huh!' Gesine scoffed. 'You could willingly have

94

slain him. Putting you in your nursery place in front of your adoring Hans—oh fie!'

Nicola said nothing and, as if satisfied she had made her point, Gesine did not pursue the subject.

'Where now?' she asked when they reached the outskirts of Montreux.

'I'm not sure. I want the Avenue Goncourt. But if you would drop me on the lake-front, there are hotels where you could wait for me, and I'd find this place where my friend works for myself,' suggested Nicola.

'Nonsense. It may be a mad distance away. We'll ask for directions, and I'll drive you and pick you up later, whenever you say.'

Once again Nicola thought agreement had to be the best policy. They enquired for the Avenue Goncourt and drove on. When they drew up at a narrow five-storeyed house, proclaimed by its rather shabby name-board to be the Pension Areuse, Gesine viewed it with distaste.

'Are you sure this is right? It looks an odd place for an ex-finishing school type to be working in. You did *say* a school-friend, didn't you?'

'Yes. And this is the right address. But don't bother to come back for me. It's only a short walk from here to the front, and I don't know how long I may need. So if you'll say where you will be, I'll come and find you when I am ready,' said Nicola, knowing she dared not risk a meeting between Gesine and a girl it was possible she might describe to Kurt.

'As you please.' They arranged a meeting-place and as soon as Gesine drove away, Nicola rang the bell of the boarding-house and walked through the open door. In an alcove of the dark hall there was a crescent-shaped reception desk and behind it sat Diane.

For a moment they stared at each other. Then Diane said on a quick breath, 'Nicola! I know what you have come for. Anton told me you would. But it's no good. You can't persuade me. I'm not going back.'

Nicola looked about her. 'Could you get some time off and take me to your room? Or come out?'

Diane shook her head. 'I can't leave the desk. Madame is out and I'm in charge. But we can talk here. It's always very quiet in the middle of the day, unless someone comes enquiring for a room——' She broke off, her face puckering with embarrassment. 'Nicola, I don't know how to thank you for what you've done for me. When Anton told me——! You know what I mean?'

Nicola took a chair under a potted palm. 'I know what you mean,' she agreed. 'And if you want to thank me, you could persuade Anton to pocket his pride and let Kurt know where you are.'

'No!' Diane's delicate jaw set firmly. 'Even out of gratitude to you, we're not going to show up yet; not until we feel we've proved Anton's good faith. *No.*'

Nicola urged patiently, 'It's too late for you to "show up" in Lausanne while the convention is on and Kurt's guests have accepted me as being you. But you ought to let him know you are safe and well, and then go back home, where no one ever need be the wiser that you left him in the cruel, reckless way you did. Make Anton see you ought to meet Kurt halfway, Diane—please!'

That somewhere in the future of Kurt's renewed courtship of Gesine, Gesine would have to be made 'the wiser' about the Lausanne trick, was a private thought Nicola did not voice. For that would be Kurt's problem, not hers. When it arose—as it must, if Kurt and Gesine were to marry—she herself would be finished with the whole fantastic affair. Back in England. And alone.

Meanwhile Diane adroitly twisted Nicola's own reasoning in order to argue that as it was too late for her to reappear in Lausanne, she was entitled to remain in hiding from Kurt for as long as she and Anton Pellerin decided would serve their purpose.

'And you don't care *that*'—Nicola snapped a finger and thumb—'for Kurt's worry about you?'

'I do mind, of course,' Diane admitted. 'But it matters less than what is at stake for Anton and me.'

'But if I hadn't shown him the letter you left for me, he wouldn't know even now why you had run away,' Nicola pointed out.

'Oh, if you hadn't been there, I'd have left a note for him instead. There wouldn't have been any point in going if I hadn't told him why.'

'And you haven't much thought either for the false position you've put *me* in, have you?'

'But I have, I have!' Diane claimed urgently. 'That was why I risked sending Anton to find out whether or not you were helping Kurt as I hoped, and when Anton told me what you had done, I couldn't feel grateful enough. I never can—— I suppose it was Kurt's idea, not yours. But you agreed to it when you needn't have done, and you did that for me?'

'When Kurt convinced me that it might save you both the scandal you had invited.' Putting it like that, Nicola dodged the admission that the magnetism of Kurt's appeal to her had had at least as much pull as her impulse to shield Diane. *Even then——!*

She made a little empty motion with her hands and stood up. 'I hoped I'd achieve more than this by seeing you,' she told Diane. 'And you are having to trust me a good deal, aren't you, to keep your whereabouts from Kurt?'

Diane nodded. 'I can't help myself. But I don't think you'll let me down. Even though—well, I was going to say that I doubt whether you know what ... love does to people. How you have to fight for it, and go on fighting. For if you did know, you would be more on my side than you are. As it is, you are half on Kurt's side too. But I've still got to trust you, and I do.'

Nicola stood up. 'Don't forget there is another side as well as yours and Kurt's—my own,' she advised drily.

'If you had let that count with you, you wouldn't have got mixed up with us at all,' Diane parried. 'Oh, are you going now? How did you come?'

'In Kurt's car. Which reminds me, you left your driving licence behind in the flat.'

'I knew I must have done. But I don't need it while I am here.'

'Which is as well, because Kurt advised me to carry it in my bag as identification, and I do. But he won't allow me to drive on it,' said Nicola.

'You mean you use your own licence?' Diane's eyes widened. 'Isn't that very risky, when you are supposed to be——?'

'I don't use either. I meant to come today by bus, but when I had no excuse for refusing to let a woman guest of Kurt's drive me, it seemed safer to accept.'

Diane gasped. 'Some woman who has come for the convention? But mightn't she tell Kurt she had brought you to see me? Who is she?'

'She is——' But an odd reluctance to discuss Kurt's and Gesine's relationship with Diane kept Nicola silent on Gesine's identity. She said instead, 'She is a woman designer in business with her cousin by marriage. But she won't have seen you, and she can only tell Kurt she brought me to Montreux to see a school-friend. She is waiting for me now at the Eurotel, so I'd better go now.'

'Yes, I suppose you must.' Diane added, 'By the way, has Kurt had to tell Aunt Agathe anything about me? She isn't at home; she is in Paris, you know.'

'Yes, and there was a letter from her for you yesterday morning. I didn't open it. I gave it to Kurt and he said he would deal with it.'

Diane shivered slightly. 'I wonder how? I hope she doesn't have to know——' She paused and came round the desk. 'Nicola, something else I want to ask. During all this, have you gained any idea of what makes Kurt tick? Why, for instance, he is so bitter and prejudiced against Anton? Or where love figures in his own life? And I don't mean affairs. He has had those, of course. But not lastingly, and I'm talking about the kind of love that *does*. Because if he had ever experienced that, surely he would be more tolerant about Anton and me? Well, wouldn't he?' she appealed.

Nicola looked away. 'You'd think so. But I'm not intimate enough with Kurt to know.'

'Oh,' Diane looked disappointed. 'You mean you don't talk much about—feelings? About yourselves?'

'Not as much as I'd expect you and Kurt to have done. After all, you have had all your lives,' Nicola pointed out.

'Ah, but it's not the same. Sisters never know as much of that side of their brothers as they show to other women, and with the age-gap between us, I know so little about Kurt that I rather hoped you——' Diane broke off and suddenly, impulsively, as they reached the hall door, cupped her hands about Nicola's face and kissed her cheek. 'But sisters do know about each other,' she muttered thickly. 'I believe they are different. They do talk; they can. I wish I had one. And if only you were mine——!' Shame-facedly she turned back into the hall, and, touched though she was, Nicola let her go.

As she went down the well-worn steps of the Pension Areuse and out under the dusty limes, she was thinking that the only way in which Diane's choked little wish could come even marginally true was the one way which would never happen for either of them.

It was on the return journey to Lausanne that Nicola realised she could not afford to let Gesine mention to Kurt that she had gone to Montreux to see a school-friend. For Kurt's mind would at once question whether she had gone genuinely as Nicola Stirling or falsely as Diane and he would certainly want to know from her why she had risked doing either.

Another bad mistake! Would she never learn? Somehow Gesine must be warned. But how? What suspicious thing would Gesine make of an appeal for her silence? Besides, the very thought of enlisting

Gesine as an ally against Kurt was one which Nicola found repugnant. But as it happened, a wry fate was to see to it that the favour of silence would be asked of her by Gesine, not the other way about.

They had gone about halfway when, after a quick glance in the driving-mirror, Gesine pulled in abruptly to the side of the road. Nicola glanced a question at her, which she answered, 'Traffic police. I must have done something wrong,' and a moment later two uniformed motor-cyclists drew up beside her window and alighted.

'Yes?'

One of the men produced a notebook; the other spoke rapidly in French with gestures and Gesine threw a look of appeal to Nicola.

Nicola interpreted, 'They say that, a couple of kilometres back, you overran a double white line. Do you remember if you did or not?'

'Oh.' Gesine bit her lip and frowned. 'Yes . . . yes, I think I remember where. So now I suppose I'll get a ticket? What a bore!'

'They want your driving licence and the car's papers. They are here'—Nicola took them from the glove compartment—'but they have a system, if you plead guilty, of a fine on the spot. I'll pay it, of course,' she offered.

'You'll do nothing of the kind.' Gesine handed over her driving licence. Nicola said, 'Madame pleads guilty to the offence.' Gesine opened her money wallet and asked, 'How much?'

'Twenty francs, *madame*.' The man with the note-book wrote a receipt; the car's papers were examined and handed back, but Gesine's driving licence was pored over, discussed and retained.

'This document is out of date, *madame*.' To prove it, it was shown to Gesine, who gasped, 'Oh no!'

'But yes, *madame*. Your licence should have been renewed in your own country a month ago. You may have it back, but you must not drive further today, nor again in our country until it is in order. You understand?'

Gesine understood. Muttering irritably, 'It's Gregor's fault. He should have reminded me,' she turned to Nicola. 'So now what do we do?' she demanded.

Nicola said, 'I don't know.' The policemen bowed, washed their hands of the problem and curveted away at speed. Gesine retorted, 'Well, I do. I hope you've got your own licence with you, for you'll have to drive.'

Nicola caught her breath. 'But——'

'Oh, nonsense,' Gesine snapped. 'Kurt can't eat you. *I'll* see that he doesn't. I'll explain—— Or shall I?' She broke off, tilting her head in thought. 'No. Look——' She turned again to Nicola. 'This licence thing makes me look rather a fool, and Kurt just might eat you—who knows? So perhaps we didn't borrow the car. We didn't go to Montreux. I didn't get caught by the cops, and you didn't disobey orders by driving the car. What about that?'

'You mean'—Nicola snatched gladly at the un-looked for reprieve—'you would rather Kurt didn't know about any of it?'

'Well, wouldn't you? After all, we don't have to lie, except by what you might call "Failure to mention", hm?'

'Very well.' But as they changed places, Nicola praying that she would invite no incriminating driving incident in her false name, Gesine had the last tart comment.

'There, you see! When it suits you to "manage" men, you are as ready to do it as the next girl. You're learning, my dear, you're learning!' she taunted.

Nicola said nothing, thankful for escape, but hating the ill chance which had put them on the same side in deceit of Kurt.

Remembering that Kurt had said he would not necessarily confide to her any steps he took to find Diane, Nicola did not expect he would tell her of the advertisement he had addressed to Anton Pellerin. But the morning after he and his party returned from Neuchâtel, he did.

Just as Anton had done, he handed her a newspaper, folded to show the item. 'I thought you might see this and query it,' he said. 'It has gone into every local and national journal in the country. I think it should bring results.'

Not needing to read it, but pretending to do so, Nicola said, 'You really expect it to?'

'If he and Diane are still in Switzerland, the chances are high that he will see it, and as I judge him to be on the watch for some overture from me, I think he won't be too long about answering it.'

'But only, surely, if you are right about him, and he is merely a fortune-hunter? If he isn't, the way you have put this'—Nicola indicated the advertisement—'is an insult I should think he would ignore.'

'Always supposing it were possible to insult his

type,' Kurt retorted.

'But do you know him well enough to judge? And anyway, it insults Diane,' she declared with spirit.

'Insults Diane? It does nothing of the sort!' Kurt looked as if his hearing had played him false.

Nicola insisted, 'Well, I think it does. For, supposing you are right that she is only Anton Pellerin's dupe, then the wording makes her sound like a kind of parcel to be bargained for. And on the other hand, if they are sincere and in love, then you insult her even more. You could at least give her the benefit of the doubt, couldn't you?'

'Of what doubt, pray? And would you say that, leaving as she did, without a word, except by proxy through you, she is entitled to much sympathy from me for her motives?'

'No, the way of her going was indefensible,' Nicola agreed. 'But she probably felt she had to. I think people who love . . . enough tend to be quite ruthless, and if Diane recognized your hard core of prejudice against Anton Pellerin, she may have known that, to fight it, she had to do something as sudden and outrageous as she did. And how can you know that it wasn't she who persuaded him, and not the other way about?'

From Kurt's long, intense look she believed she might have given him pause. But his reply, when it came, was touched by irrelevance. 'You know, for one as unscathed by her affairs as you claim to be, I shouldn't expect you to know very much about the rashness of "loving enough",' he commented.

Nicola looked away. 'Wouldn't you? Not even in theory?' she countered.

He laughed shortly. 'Ah, theory! I'll allow you theory. It was your experience I was calling in question. Speak from theory only—and you can't blame your audience if it doesn't listen.'

'So you aren't listening,' she stated flatly.

'To your argument, no. Only to a loyalty to Diane which makes me feel that in any issue I cared about passionately, I'd give a very great deal to have you on my side.'

Again she dropped her eyes before the intensity of his look. 'Well, aren't I on your side—in this?' she queried.

He shook his head. 'Not wholeheartedly. You are still more than half on Diane's, aren't you?'

She wished she could confess the extent to which they were tearing her loyalty between them. Instead she said:

'Only because I think I see where you are both wrong. And to me your reasoning seems twisted. For instance, aren't you judging Anton Pellerin in much the same unjust way you were judged when you first courted Madame Silber? From what you have told me about that, you were up against a prejudice you couldn't fight——'

'Correction—"was too proud to fight".—then or later. However—"twisted"? So——! If you consider the two cases are parallel, perhaps you also think I could be hounding Pellerin in the one, out of some belated revenge for the other?'

Nicola bit her lip. 'I'd hate to believe you capable of it.'

'But supposing I were—and I gather you think I might be—you'd want no further part in the whole thing?'

Shamed by his insight into the nagging doubt in her mind, she said dully, 'I've no choice. I already have a part in it. I came into it with my eyes open, and I can't let you down.'

'In other words, making a martyrdom of your staying?' he demanded harshly. 'I assure you, there's no need!'

She flinched. 'Making a duty of my staying. There's a difference,' she said, prepared to gather her forces against his retort, however sarcastic or withering it might be.

When it came it was neither. With that switch from arrogance to diffidence which she knew was one facet of his attraction for her, he said quietly, 'So there is. I'm sorry. And since your duty is all I've the right to ask of you, believe me, I'm grateful for that.'

*All he had the right to ask.* Ah, if only he knew how much, much more she was willing to give!,

## CHAPTER SIX

As the days passed, the social tempo of the convention quickened. Almost every evening there were parties given variously by the foreign buyers; the more pretentious ones taking place in the Palais de Beaulieu, the more intimate in the hosts' hotels.

Gregor Silber and Gesine had already given one of the latter when Kurt told Nicola they were both invited to another. The Silbers had made other friends at the Beau Rivage, and they proposed to show them hospitality as well as to the cosmopolitan members of Kurt's party.

'It promises to be a rather bigger affair than the last,' Kurt remarked. 'By the way, how is your wardrobe for this sort of thing? Is it beginning to feel the strain?'

In fact it was. Nicola had done her best by switching dress-accessories—bags, belts, hair ornaments—but at too many functions of the same nature as each other her three cocktail outfits had appeared too often. But reluctant to admit as much, she parried Kurt's question. 'Why? Do you think it is showing signs of wear and tear?'

'I hadn't noticed it. To me, you do your part all the credit I could ask. But I have an idea you haven't obeyed orders. You haven't passed me any bills for clothes to date, have you? Why not?' he asked.

'I haven't incurred any. I—preferred not to.'

'And I prefer that you should; that Diane Thesige should be seen to spend some Thesige money in Lausanne which is playing its part in promoting Thesige business. So I expect you to quash your personal scruples with our prestige in view, do you see? I daresay you know which are the best dress salons here by now, don't you? If not, Gesine is sure to. Ring her and ask.'

'I'd rather you rang her,' Nicola said.

'Nonsense, it's women's gossip. She'll be flattered. Ring her, ask her for an address or two and tell her I'm taking you shopping.' He paused to calculate times. 'I'm due at the Palais now for an hour, but I'll meet you at the Lausanne-Palace bar at eleven. You will be there?'

When she arrived he was not yet there. But the American Bar at the Lausanne-Palace, being as central a rendezvous as any, was a favourite meeting-place for the delegates, and as Nicola crossed to a table, Hans Durer detached himself from a group and came to join her.

'You are alone?' he asked in surprise.

'Not really. I'm meeting Kurt.'

'Oh—— But I may stay until he comes? And you'll have a drink with me—please?' he begged.

She told him her choice and he signalled a waiter. She asked him if he were going to the Silbers' party and he said he was.

'You too, of course? You and your brother?'

When Nicola said Yes, he sighed, fingering the stem of his glass. 'There's so little time left now. After the Show at the Palais we shall all be parting and going home. Everyone scattering—— And any spare time there is now seems to be filled to its last minute with duty contacts and parties which, since one just *might* do some business at them, one doesn't care to escape.' He paused and threw Nicola a glance. 'Or aren't any of them duty affairs to you? I suppose you enjoy them all?'

She smiled. 'Not all of them. Especially when there are more than one in an evening.'

He agreed gloomily, 'As there have been. And you are always so much in demand that I've hardly exchanged a word with you since the night you let me drive you to Vevey and Chillon.'

But Nicola would not have that. 'Oh, come!' she urged. 'Somewhere or other, we've met each other nearly every day, and *I* remember talking to *you*.'

'Ah, but almost always in a crowd; other people sharing you. Not like——' He broke off to add ·diffidently, 'I suppose I mustn't ask for one more evening with you before——? But no, I see in your face that you are going to refuse!'

In fact she wanted badly to accept. From the web of love with no future, and secrecy and intrigue in which she was caught, an hour or two in his gentle company should prove a brief escape. Yet it wasn't as simple as that—two people enjoying a relaxed evening together. For Hans was attracted by her, she sensed, and even his shy diffidence was a kind of courtship in its way. And she had promised Kurt she wouldn't encourage him——

She said, 'I'd like very much to say yes, and perhaps I can. But it's rather difficult——' From the corner of her eye she saw Kurt approaching, and at the same time Hans saw him too.

'I've been asking your sister whether she could spare me another evening some time. Or rather, whether you could spare her to me perhaps,' he told Kurt.

Kurt looked from him to Nicola. 'Can I?' he asked.

Feeling that his question had held a warning against eagerness to encourage Hans, she made her reply non-committal. 'It's for you to say,' she told him.

'Yes, well——' Kurt frowned in calculation. 'What about Thursday? Or no, that's the night we're all going over to Sion for "Son et Lumière". Friday, then? Even if someone lays on a party beforehand, you'll dine at the villa on Friday, I hope?' he asked Hans.

Though Nicola guessed that a threesome for dinner was not what Hans had had in mind, he snatched at the suggestion, as at the proverbial straw.

'Friday? Thank you. I shall look forward to that,' he said, and stood, with a formal bow for Nicola as she and Kurt went out.

In the car she gave Kurt the first of the addresses Gesine had recommended. ('Go to town, my dear, while you've the chance,' Gesine had advised her mockingly. 'What else are wealthy brothers *for*?') Kurt nodded approval. 'Yes, Fabriola—it has a reputation that has reached even me,' he said. He edged the car out from the kerb. 'A biddable lad, your Hans. I congratulate you on how you've trained him,' he commented.

Nicola had to bite back a tart retort to that. 'That was Hans Durer being his natural, nice self. Except at people's parties, I haven't been alone with him since the night he took me out. He's had no training of any kind from me,' she said.

110

'Then he is blessed with a particularly fine intuition, since he appears to have learned to be grateful for mere crumbs from you. Which is just as well, isn't it—in the circumstances?' Kurt insinuated.

'Meaning that, supposing he had asked for more, or that I had encouraged him or responded, that would have been inconvenient, if not even—dangerous for us? Yes, so you said once before, and I don't need warning again, thank you. Hans is a genuine person whom I like very much, from the little I know of him——'

Kurt cut in, '—From the little I've allowed you to know of him, you would have liked to say, perhaps?'

'Perhaps.' (He deserved that!) Nicola went on, 'Anyway, to date there has been no more than liking between us. No danger at all, I assure you.'

Kurt's glance went quickly sideways, then back to the street and the traffic. Almost mildly he said, 'We're not quite on the same beam. No new warning was intended. My congratulations were—to "*La Belle Dame Sans Merci*"—to a certain lovely, cool lady without too much compassion or after-regret—who patently needs no advice from me on how to manage men or how to keep them at their proper distance! She knows it all already, doesn't she?'

Nicola swallowed hard. 'By "La Belle Dame", I take it you mean me?' she said.

Another swift glance her way. 'Who else?' As he spoke Kurt was drawing in to a kerb at an overhead scarlet-fringed canopy leading to a scarlet and gold doorway inscribed 'Fabriola'. A uniformed doorman sprang to open the car door, but Kurt kept him wait-

111

ing. He laid a hand gently and briefly on Nicola's knee.

'Anyway,' he queried, 'wasn't it for Hans's own sake that we agreed earlier that it wouldn't do? And if you like him as much as you claim, you wouldn't want him wantonly hurt, would you?'

Wordlessly she shook her head, and he let her go.

He was right, of course. She knew as well as he that Hans mustn't be allowed to fall for a girl-who-never-was; for a Diane Thesige who didn't exist. And with that sincere plea for Hans he had been able, as always, to disarm her. Going ahead of him as the doorman ushered them with a flourish into the salon, she was wondering bleakly where her complete surrender to his magnetism was going to stop. As it must, if she were ever to be free of loving him; free to forget him and to love elsewhere.

An hour later they were bowed out of the salon, followed by the doorman carrying Kurt's purchases to the car. He had shown himself a patient and shrewd critic of every outfit Nicola had tried on, and when she had selected two, he asked that she be shown evening bags and Italian-made sandals to go with each.

He was not known personally and there was a moment of embarrassment when the head saleswoman, addressing Nicola formally as 'Madame', assumed by her manner that Kurt was buying clothes for her as his wife. As soon as Nicola realised this, she looked an appeal to him which, to her surprise, he rejected with a slight shake of his head.

When they were briefly alone while the woman went to ascertain that a fitting-room was free, he explained himself.

'There's no need to advertise our relationship,' he said. 'We are only birds of passage, paying cash. And I'd judge that in a chi-chi establishment like this, wives have a shade more cachet than mere sisters.'

*Or impostors?* was Nicola's inevitable thought, and before they left there was another pinprick of chagrin in store for her, this time invited by a rash word of her own.

She had said she had everything she wanted and was pleased, when suddenly the saleswoman pleaded, 'Please, *madame*? Just one moment more? A fancy of mine——' and disappeared through a silver-curtained archway to return with an evening-dressed wig on a model head.

In its way it was a lovely thing—a silken fall of loose curls of exactly Nicola's own colouring, mounted on a velvet and diamanté-studded bandeau. The woman stroked it reverently, draping its length over her hand. 'For the evening affair, *madame*. All the mode. Me, as soon as I think of it, I tell myself it is *you*. You like it, *madame*? You will try it on?'

Alone, Nicola might have been tempted. But with Kurt looking on, she was shy. She shook her head. 'It's lovely, I agree. But I've never worn one. I don't think—— That is, I'm sure I should feel, wearing it, that I was in disguise——'

As soon as she had uttered the word, with its unfortunate slant of meaning for herself and Kurt, she saw it had not escaped him. His voice clashing with the saleswoman's, he said coolly, 'And what's wrong with a bit of disguise—in a good cause?' And she, glancing covertly at him—'You see, *madame*? Monsieur

113

approves! So you will try on our little piece of nonsense to please him, if not to please me?'

'Very well.'

A younger girl, bewigged herself, was summoned from beyond the archway; Nicola was seated before a mirror; the girl deftly arranged the wig to blend with the line of her hair, and standing back to view her handiwork, added her own quota of persuasion.

'In our profession, *madame*, we tell each other that to wear a new wig is as good for the morale as an invitation to an exciting *bal masqué*. One becomes a different person. Even one's friends look ... and have to look again. And to feel a little unknown ... tantalisingly *incognita*, if only for an evening, that is always romantic, as you will find.'

Nicola caught her breath, and heard Kurt's short laugh.

'You are a good saleswoman,' he told the girl. 'You know how to appeal. Madame will take the wig—even though she sometimes likes to pretend she is entirely indifferent to romance.'

The younger girl smiled and the older woman affected wide-eyed shock at that. 'Ah no, *monsieur*! That is just a little trick Madame likes to play on you. So young, so charming—and caring nothing for romance? No, never!'

Upon which they had both joined in conspiratorial laughter; Kurt had produced his wallet again; the wig was boxed and added to the other parcels and Kurt and Nicola had left.

Kurt stopped the packages from being put into his car, telling the man, 'Madame and I are going different ways, so call a taxi for her, will you, and put the things into it.' He added to Nicola, 'I may not be back until it is time to change, this evening, and I daresay you'll want to stage a private dress-rehearsal. And I hope you'll decide to wear that wig at Gesine's party. Diane would need no persuasion, I know.'

When they arrived there was already a crowd in the room, many of whom they knew, though as many again were strangers.

'Trust Gesine to collect a larger circle of acquaintances than any other woman in a given time,' Kurt remarked drily. He looked about him. 'Let's see— whom shall we join until she happens to circulate this way and do some introductions?'

Nicola nodded in the direction of the wife of one of the American buyers. 'Mrs Godefroy seems to be alone,' she said. 'Or over there is Herr Blume——'

'Who is about to be buttonholed by Mynheer "Jewelled Movement" ' (the party's nickname for an earnest Dutchman of dedicated watchmaking mind). Kurt shook his head. 'I think I prefer to squire Mrs Godefroy, and we'll attract another male for you.'

This latter was to be Gregor Silber, apologising for not having welcomed them when they came in, but it was not until some time and considerable 'circulation' later that Gesine lifted a hand to Nicola from across the room, adding a resigned shrug to indicate that for the moment she was too much engaged to come over.

Nor did she come when the group of which she was the centre began to break up and to re-form elsewhere. Then she stood, talking and laughing alone with a young man whom Nicola did not know, though she had the impression that for at least some of the time they were facing her, she was the subject of their talk.

She could not have said why, except through the same sixth sense that is aware of, without needing to meet, a watching eye. By then she had met and was alone with Hans, who had certainly been one of those to 'look . . . and look again' at her in waterlily green Italian silk and the dark transfiguring sweep of the wig.

At first sight of her he had gasped, his eager eyes travelling over her, confirming the admiration of his, 'Diane! How lovely you look! I——'

'Don't say you wouldn't have known me,' she teased. 'For that wouldn't be a compliment.'

'Which are all I have—compliments,' he said. 'And of course I should know you—anywhere, dressed anyhow. And all my life long, Diane. For ever——'

At the deep sincerity in his voice she blushed, at a loss for a reply, knowing that she mustn't hurt him with another flippancy like her first. He went on urgently, 'Diane, it isn't possible here. But on Friday, when I come to dinner at the villa, I shall find some chance to talk to you? I must, please. Say yes?'

She shrank a little. But—'Yes. Yes, of course,' she told him. (What else could she say?) Then Gesine was approaching, her companion with her, and Gesine, taking both her hands and holding her at arm's length, was saying, 'Diane, my sweet! What a charming tribute to my party—to make yourself such an enchanting picture for it! Or'—a sidelong glance at Hans—'wasn't it perhaps *all* for me? However, no matter. Here is someone I want you to meet. He is English, a professional journalist, who is taking a few days' holiday before he is due to cover the Porcelain Fair next week. Diane, Mr Roy Forsett. And now perhaps you can settle an argument for us. He has been telling me he is pretty sure he has met you before, which I think unlikely, though if he has I expect you'll know?'

Dangerous ground. Nicola felt her wrist quiver with apprehension as she offered her hand to the stranger. Speaking English, as Gesine usually did, she said, 'Really? I don't think Mr Forsett and I have met anywhere. If we have, I don't remember it at all.'

She met the critical scrutiny of his cold, light eyes; saw them assess her features, her hair, her figure. 'I hardly expected you would, *mademoiselle*,' he said. 'You see, it was only at a distance that I believe I saw you, and we didn't speak. But on just one occasion in Scotland last winter—weren't you there?'

So that was it! By the most remote of chances she would have thought she had to fear, she was being claimed, not as Diane, but in her own right as Nicola Stirling. What then? A downright lie? No, a half-truth was easier, and Scotland was a big country . . . She nodded. 'Yes, I was in Scotland for a little while,' she admitted. 'But——'

Roy Forsett turned to Gesine. 'There, you see!' Back again to Nicola. 'As I thought. So I was right, and I could have seen you in'—a moment's pause—'in Edinburgh in January?'

She drew a long breath of relief. Knowing she had never seen him before, she could tell the truth now about her few days as temporary secretary to a body of London stationers in conference in Glasgow.

'I'm sorry, no,' she said. 'I only went to Glasgow. I

didn't visit Edinburgh at all.'

The light eyes and the pale brows above them affected surprise and shock. 'You went to Scotland on a visit, *mademoiselle*, and only took in Glasgow, without touching on its Edinburgh or its mountains or its lakes? Honestly! For shame! You certainly must go again and put that record straight as soon as you can.'

'Yes, mustn't I?' she began, cutting across Gesine's little crow of triumph.

'There!' she claimed to her companion in her turn. 'We should have had money on it, my friend! But'—another meaning glance shared between Nicola and Hans—'I have an idea we are just a shade *de trop* here. So come along. Somewhere around there's a rather enchanting American redhead I met in the bar only this morning. You might try convincing *her* you once met her in St. Louis or Cincinnatti or wherever——' With which she bore Roy Forsett off, leaving Nicola and Hans alone.

Hans scowled. 'That type seemed very sure of himself—at first,' he said. 'But you had never seen him before, had you?'

'Never in my life, so far as I know.'

'Then why?' puzzled Hans. 'It was just an excuse to meet you? Could that be it?'

'I doubt it. When men try that, they usually march up and say it to your face, not to a third person, I've found.'

'And men have tried it on you—to your face?' he queried jealously.

Nicola laughed. 'I don't suppose there's a girl in your country or mine who hasn't been at the receiving end of it at one time or another. But don't worry. Most of us have ways of brushing it off.'

'I hope so indeed. It is—cheap,' said Hans critically.

But though they tacitly dismissed the subject there, the incident stayed to rankle at the back of Nicola's mind.

There had been something about it which rang not quite true, either as a genuine mistake on the man's part or, as Hans had suggested, as a roundabout way of getting to know her. Try as she would, she could not lay a finger on the point where its falsity lay. But worrying about it was to spoil the rest of the evening and to keep her fitfully awake that night.

Not without reason, as she was to learn too soon. The next morning, as she was about to call Gesine to thank her on her own and Kurt's behalf for the party, the telephone rang and Gesine was on the line.

'Diane?'

'Yes. You beat me to it. I was just going to ring you. Kurt wanted me to tell you how much we enjoyed the party.'

'That's all right. He told me so—quite adequately —last night before he left. But it's you I want this morning. Could you come round to see me?'

Nicola hesitated. 'I'm supposed to be finding out who wants to go over to Sion on Thursday night. But yes, I could, I suppose. When?'

'As soon as possible. I'll wait in for you. Come to my room.'

'Very well.' Her curiosity as yet untouched by alarm, she added, 'What is it all about?'

There was a pregnant silence. Then Gesine's husky voice drawled, 'Just something rather important—quite important, in fact—to us both and to someone else. I'll expect you to come.' She rang off, leaving Nicola to cradle her own receiver and to stare down at it with unfocussed eyes; taking in its message of threat only by degrees. For there *had* been menace in Gesine's last words. The rapiers, ostensibly sheathed for some time now, were out for use again. Why?

She was not to be left long in doubt. This time, in Gesine's room there was no tray of drinks and after a cool nod of greeting, Gesine went straight to the point.

'And so, Miss *Nicola Stirling*'—she emphasised each name firmly—'what are you and my good friend Kurt Thesige up to, one wonders? Or should it be possible to guess? Suppose you tell me?'

It was hopeless to pretend righteous surprise. Nicola knew that her involuntary start at the sound of her name had already betrayed her. She answered Gesine's question, 'I shouldn't dream of making you guess the details of why I'm passing as Kurt's sister for the moment. What do you want to know? That is,' she added in cornered defiance, 'if you consider you have the right to question me about a matter that's quite private between Kurt and me?'

Gesine tilted an enquiring head. 'Do you know,' she drawled, 'I'd have said I had the right of any of your friends whom you've chosen to hoodwink with this stupid masquerade? But I won't embarrass you by demanding explanations. I'll tell you instead. Though I confess defeat as to why you and Kurt, if you wanted a clandestine week or two together, couldn't have signed in at some back-street hotel as, say, Monsieur and Madame Dupont, instead of this virtuous parade! And something else I don't quite understand—how did you induce real little sister Diane to play?'

For a moment Nicola was speechless. Then she stammered, 'You think that I——? That *Kurt* and I——?'

'What else? After all, a furnished luxury villa; staff probably engaged through an agency; a pleasant social scene and—who knows?—even the appalling risk you run, adding a certain piquancy. The only snag, to an outsider, being Diane. And you seem to have dealt successfully with that?'

Her outraged shock reducing her almost to entreaty, Nicola heard herself clamour, 'But you've got it all wrong! *Really!* It was for Diane, not——! Oh, you can't think there's been anything like—that between Kurt and me! He doesn't mean a—a thing to me in that way.'

Gesine shrugged. 'If you say so. Though it's always a shade suspicious, didn't you know, to protest too much?'

Nicola claimed wildly, 'I'm not just protesting. And anyway, I don't mean a thing to Kurt.'

There was a small silence. Then—'Well, not *permanently*, perhaps,' Gesine said, her tone a studied insult. She went on, 'And so I jumped to too-hasty conclusions? It wasn't for the purpose of a cosy little passing affair, but for Diane's sake, you say? How so?'

'Because after Kurt had brought her here to act as his hostess for the convention, she ran away with a man Kurt had the power to forbid her to marry. That left Kurt without a hostess and, far worse, with a possible scandal neither his business nor his care for Diane's reputation could afford. She left from a flat they had taken for a couple of nights before going to the villa. I happened to be at the flat; she left me to break the news to Kurt and——'

The story came out in such a torrent of urgent words that Gesine had no choice but to listen in silence. At the end she nodded, her eyes narrowing in calculation. 'Quite the cloak-and-dagger intrigue,' she commented. 'And promising success to date, but for that unfortunate chance that brought young Forsett to my party last night, hm?'

Nicola stared. 'That's how you knew my name? He told you? But he couldn't have recognised me. I never met him in Edinburgh as he claimed.'

Gesine smiled thinly. 'He's an astute lad. He trapped you with "Edinburgh" into admitting to "Glasgow"—which is where he did see you at the time you said.'

Nicola remembered his hesitation over the word Edinburgh. So that was the unheeded clue which had fretted her mind last night! She said dully, 'I see,' and Gesine went on:

'He was on an assignment at the hotel where you were doing—oh, whatever you do for a living—for a batch of businessmen. He had time on his hands; he asked one of them your name, but before he could make a pass, your party had booked out. At first he wasn't too sure about you. He said your hair was different. But I told him to use his eyes—you were wearing a hair-piece. And after he had spoken to you, he told *me* I should have used my ears—that your English accent was far too perfect for you to be Swiss.

Though as if I'd know, considering I haven't set foot in the dreary country for years,' she concluded, reaching nonchalantly for a cigarette.

Nicola watched its glow. 'And now you know all about me, what do you propose to do?' she asked.

'Do?' Gesine's hand wafted smoke from before her face. 'Why should I "do" anything about it?'

'Because,' Nicola said carefully, 'I doubt if you would have made such an importance of telling me you knew, if you hadn't plans to use it. And you said "important for someone else". Did that mean—Kurt?'

'Naturally Kurt—who else? But that's not to say I mean to do anything active—for the moment—to publish a story that you have both been at such pains to keep from coming out. I could see that it got around, of course. Roy Forsett isn't a journalist for nothing—— But though I mean to have the truth from you, it was rather different from what I expected, and I see no urgency to use it—yet.'

'Though, if the truth had been that Kurt and I were having an affair, you wouldn't have hesitated to use it?'

'Mm, perhaps. Though even then I might have chosen to keep it as a weapon up my sleeve for a while. For use if necessary. If not, not.'

'To use against Kurt—who was in love with you, and who hasn't married anyone else, and who is courting you again now? And against Diane Thesige who has never done you any harm? In pity's name, *why*?' Nicola demanded, meaning the word 'pity' with all her heart.

'Why?' Gesine echoed. 'Because—for a minor

reason or two—— I object to Kurt's having enlisted a little wage-slave like you to make a fool of his friends, including me. I didn't relish either the suspicion that he was your lover, short-lived though that idea was. But for a major reason—by the way, what do *you* know about his "courting" me. Tch! What a dated word, my dear! Where *did* you dig it up?'

'It's a lovely word—or should be,' Nicola contradicted. 'Because *he* has told me as much and—on the launch, coming back from Evian—your cousin Gregor and I saw you in his arms.'

'*Gregor* did? Oh dear, poor man! And I hoped he hadn't realised the work I've been putting in on Kurt. And since we are being frank, it is proving to be work, believe me.'

'You surprise me. I'd have said you hadn't had to want for every possible attention from him since you came,' Nicola returned tartly.

'Attention?' Gesine scoffed. 'What's mere attention worth? I can get all I want of that from Gregor or almost any other man I know. Which brings me to my chief reason for keeping a little revenge of my own in reserve against Kurt's long-standing revenge against me for having turned him down when he was mine for the asking. Oh, he wants me, and he means to have me, if only to satisfy his pride of possession, and he's grown a lot of that since we last met. But while he has this love–hate thing for me that means to make me pay for jilting him five years ago, he could find to his cost that I'm in a position to dictate terms and timing too. You see?'

Nicola agreed, 'I see. You're glad to know what you have learnt about all this, so that, if necessary, you can use your promise of silence as a kind of lever against Kurt? But there's a rather unpleasant word for that, isn't there? It's—blackmail.'

'Only if I make use of the story, and I may not have to.'

'Though if Kurt doesn't ask you to marry him as soon as you think he should, you might? You wouldn't care what the story could do to his position or to Diane's reputation or even to me?'

Gesine rose and crossed to her dressing-table, seating herself with her back to Nicola as if in dismissal. She began to examine her nails and to use a file lightly on their tips. 'Do you know, I can't bring myself to be very much concerned about you? Whenever Kurt has finished with you—either in his own time or mine—I'm sure he'll pay you handsomely. As for him and Diane, we shall just have to hope that he won't need too much persuasion, shan't we?' she said.

# CHAPTER SEVEN

SEETHING with impotent anger, Nicola got herself out of the room and out of the hotel, vowing inwardly that only her duty to Kurt would allow her to show Gesine any cordiality ever again. They would have to meet, of course, and outwardly their relationship must not have altered. But she would keep even ordinary politeness to a minimum; more, she could not manage.

Meanwhile was there anything she could do to turn the edge of Gesine's threat? Nothing, short of telling Kurt that two other people in Lausanne, one of them Gesine, knew their secret. And if he loved Gesine, how would his loyalty to her react to that? If he believed the story—and he might not—he could either tell Gesine and Roy Forsett to do their worst, courting the risk that they might do it, or he could buy his own good name and Diane's by agreeing to Gesine's cynical terms.

Both possibilities filled Nicola with shame for him. By the one he would lose mastery of a situation he had handled with power so far; the other called for a sacrifice that shouldn't be asked of him. That she herself believed his high-handed condemnation of Diane to be wrong had nothing at all to do with it, she argued. She had gone along with him in the first place and, loving him now, she was prepared to go further . . . all the way. And so, by no word or action of hers, was she going to precipitate a crisis which might never happen. *Need* never happen at all, if only either Diane or Kurt would relent before the very little time that was left to them ran out. And for one thing she must be thankful, she supposed. Evidently Gesine had not added two and two, connecting the 'school-friend' in Montreux with Diane. So far as Nicola had allowed her to think, Nicola knew no more of Diane's whereabouts than did Kurt. Which was as well, since Gesine would have made a double-edged weapon of the knowledge, Nicola had little doubt.

On her way back to the villa she debated making another plea of her own to Diane, but decided it was hopeless. She wondered yet again, as she always did every morning when the post came, whether Anton Pellerin was going to respond to Kurt's advertisement. Of course he hadn't so far, or Kurt would have told her. But there was no harm in hoping, even if there was no future to it.

Back at the villa she forced herself to concentrate on telephoning round, making up the list of their guests for the visit to Sion. Kurt came in to luncheon. She reported the results of her task; they discussed Gesine's party; she told him that Gesine had rung, forestalling her own 'thank you' for it. But she said nothing about Gesine's summons to her, and she and Kurt parted at the end of the meal, he to drive back to Neuchâtel, where he would be spending the night, she to join a swimming party down at La Harpe.

The trip to Sion, ninety kilometres or so into the heart of the Valais country, would be the party's last social occasion before the climax of the exhibition at the Palais de Beaulieu. Kurt had planned that they should arrive in time to explore the historic old market town before the fall of dusk which would herald the performance of Son et Lumière among the ruins of the bishop's palace atop craggy Tourbillon, one of Sion's twin rocks, both Tourbillon and Valère rising from the plain in steep fairytale contours, necklaced about by hairpin paths.

The cars were parked and people separated into twos and threes to wander round the picturesque streets, to linger in the produce market at stalls selling flowers and fat bundles of asparagus and dew-fresh early strawberries, before climbing up to view the grim stone and polished carvings of Valère's fortified church.

Afterwards they all met for drinks in the vine-covered courtyard of the inn where they were to return for supper before driving back to Lausanne. By the time they were ready for the tortuous climb up Tourbillon it was fully dark and from below, the lights that winked out from Tourbillon and Valère appeared only a little less distant than the stars. Far up Tourbillon, the floodlighting at the summit defied the stars, showing the ruined stonework of the palace in sharp white outline against the black of the sky.

The performance, by professional actors and musicians, backed in the crowd scenes by townsfolk, played out the long history of the region since Saracen hordes, fleeing from the crusading armies, had run for shelter in the Alpine heights and had stayed to mix with the valley people, peacefully self-supported by their crops, their livestock and their homecrafts except when the spring torrents from the mountains swelled the Rhône to vicious, greedy flood, or when every able-bodied man was press-ganged by his overlords into wars of baron against baron, State against State.

Because disaster is news and peace is not, it was mostly of battles and fleeing refugees and pillage and short-lived victories that the Sion pageant told. Tourbillon and Valère and, nearby, almost impregnable Isérables had all been strongholds for guerilla snipers in their time, and the re-enacted clashes for possession of them were some of the most exciting sequences of the evening's spectacle.

One of them was to have a personal point for Nicola. It was a scene in which a puny band of homespun Swiss archers on the ramparts of Tourbillon were embattled by a host of Austrian invaders below. In their favour the archers had only the courage of desperation and the superior height of their vantage-point, but the scene showed them using their bows to such swift, deadly purpose that the enemy were seen to be routed. The lights trained on them were darkened and illumined again to show their abandoned 'dead' and the survivors straggling away downhill; there was a blare of triumphant music for the victorious bowmen and Kurt, sitting behind Nicola, touched her on the shoulder and bent to her ear.

'You see what a really well-feathered shaft can do?' he murmured, and could not know, as she turned her head and nodded in understanding, how he had wrung her heart.

The night was calm and still, the backcloth of the sky a blue-black velvet. At the end of the performance the players stayed to take their applause and to be patient with the general clamour that they pose for flashlight pictures to be taken.

For a time, all over the arena, magnesium flared sporadically. Then the audience pronounced itself satisfied, the players bowed and waved au revoir and the stage was darkened for the last time.

As before, for the walk down to the inn, Kurt's party broke up. He and Hans made a foursome with Nicola and Mrs Godefroy, the men leading the way on the narrow flights of worn steps and uneven pathways where only two could go abreast.

Suddenly Kurt halted and turned with a 'Pff!' of annoyance. 'I've left my exposure meter behind. I'll have to go back for it,' he explained.

The other three sympathised. 'Of course. Shall we wait for you?'

'No, go on down without me. I shan't be long.' As if on an impulse he offered a hand to Nicola. 'Come back with me?' he invited.

She hesitated, half suspecting he was intent on separating her from Hans. But at Mrs Godefroy's playful urging, 'Say, I'd go with him if I were you, honey. Most of the actors must still be up there and there were quite a few good-looking dollies in the cast!' she laughed, turned with Kurt and played her part.

'I'll see he doesn't get hooked by one of them,' she promised Mrs Godefroy, adding to Hans, 'Keep a place for me at your table, won't you?', to which he agreed gravely, 'But of course.'

On the way up they met late stragglers from the audience and parties of the cast and the orchestra coming down. Frequently Kurt had to answer their kindly enquiries as to his errand. But by the time they reached the summit they seemed to have met the last of them. The arena itself was dark and deserted, only the ruined stonework still floodlit from lamps far below.

Kurt found his seat and the abandoned exposure meter and he and Nicola began to retrace their steps. They had not gone far when an unearthly, long-drawn shriek from behind and above them cut across the silence, causing Nicola to start in terror and to shrink into a V-niche in the breast-high parapet which bordered the pathway on its sheer side.

Instantly Kurt's arm went round her and he was laughing down into her startled face. 'Only a screech-owl wooing the night. What did you think it was—a sheeted ghost from down the centuries?' he teased.

She laughed back at him, feeling incredibly foolish. 'An owl! Of course! Where? On top of the ruins? But what a bloodcurdling yell!'

Kurt retorted, 'Madame Hibou wouldn't agree with you. To her it's a love-call, no less. And look, we've disturbed Monsieur himself now. He's going to find her. Hear his wings? See him? *There!* No, *chérie*, there—— Ah, you've lost him. He's swooped down nearly to river level. You won't be able to pick him out now.'

'Oh dear, I wish I'd seen him. I only *felt* him leave. Do you think he has gone to join Mrs Owl, wherever she is?'

'One hopes so. Happy ending for owls.'

As Nicola had put her question she had straightened from craning down over the rampart, thrusting back her hair as she did so. But a lock fell forward again and Kurt released her in order to anchor it behind her ear.

They faced each other, very close in the confines of the V. For Nicola it was an electric moment of temptation. Headily, dangerously, she *wanted* to move closer still ... into his arms, at whatever the cost in shame and rejection. He would make no gesture towards her——

But suddenly he was muttering thickly, 'You tempt me—and you shouldn't. What do you think I'm made of?' Then, his hands reaching out to cup her face from temple to jaw, he found her lips with his own, kissed her long and hard, demanding her response, then held her back from him, letting his hands drop to her shoulders and away.

He turned back to the parapet and stared out over the dark valley. When he took out his case and lit a cigarette, she felt a petty relief for her pride in noticing that his fingers were shaking. So he was upset too? Good——

Hating herself for taking out her pain on him, she accused him unsteadily, 'That was pretty meaningless, wasn't it? Just because, I daresay, because you were feeling—amorous—and I happened to be here? S-supposing we had been seen?'

He did not look at her. 'We weren't seen,' he said. 'Just as well, though it was hardly fair to trade on that. Besides, between you and me, placed as we are, it was a—a nonsense. No point or reason for it at all.'

He started irritably at that. 'All right, it was a nonsense. But *mon Dieu,* how you worry away at a mere kiss as a dog worries a bone! The whys, the wherefores, the post-mortems!' He paused and turned to look her over almost insolently. 'And all quite out of character, I'd have said, with the image of someone

132

who, on her own showing, can brush off the overtures of flirtatious males at a touch! Leave it, can't you? Or can't you leave it? Do you mean to force me to spell it out, letter by letter?'

Without knowing it, he had put his finger on the raw of her perverse need to nag him into explaining his impulse. But at the thought that perhaps he had sensed her own invitation; had accepted in chivalry's name, no more, and now was trying to cover up for her, she said less captiously, 'I only wondered. It was just so very unexpected, when we aren't at all on that kind of terms.'

'Terms! Are ours so cut-and-dried that there's no place in them for the cavalier impulse, hm? Nor for—curiosity, which, since you insist, was what sparked off my assault. Satisfied?'

With every word he spoke he killed her hope that, if only momentarily, he had wanted her as she had wanted him. She said bleakly, 'I see. "Curiosity." The same you felt towards Gesine Silber as soon as you saw her again? And kissed her to find out?'

'Not at all the same thing,' he retorted. 'I had once been in love with Gesine, and I needed to rediscover her. You, I had a passing urge to *dis*cover—an entirely different process. And when only curiosity is afoot, it's quite possible to feel it for more than one woman, you know.'

Nicola said again, 'I see. And what did your passing urge discover about me?'

Before he replied Kurt levered himself from the parapet, stubbed out his cigarette and faced downhill. 'Precisely nothing,' he said. 'Or nothing I didn't suspect before.' And then, as her belated pride or fear of what she might hear, warned her against questioning him further, he laughed shortly. 'Don't worry,' he said. 'Your citadel remains unbreached by any impertinent probing of mine. It'll survive one isolated, uninvited kiss, I daresay.' And then, briskly, 'It's time we were on our way. If we dally any longer we're going to be missed.'

It was their cue for taking up the threads of normality again. They talked about the journey from Lausanne and the evening's performance and Sion, and just before they reached the inn Kurt said, 'You realise, don't you, that I can't have you around at the Exhibition? The day before it, workmen from the home factories will be setting up our stands, and salesmen who know Diane will be manning them. I'll think of a plausible reason for your being unable to attend, and you'll have to go away for a couple of days. Where would you like to go?'

'I don't know. It doesn't matter. Say, Geneva?' Nicola suggested.

'Very well. I'll book you in at the Hotel de La Paix. I'll come over and bring you back in time to speed our guests on their various homeward ways. I shall stay on in Lausanne myself for a while, but I can free you as soon as you like after the last of them have gone.'

'And what shall I tell people about why I shan't be at the Exhibition?'

'Tell them nothing for now. They'll expect you to be there, and your absence must be due to some last-minute, more urgent call on you. Leave it to me. I'll brief you before you have to go.'

'Very well.' As they reached the inn and joined the gay, noisy parties at the supper tables, Nicola was counting the days. Less than a week now, and for her the whole fantastic scene would be over, and nothing solved between Diane and Kurt. Only—for as long as Gesine kept silent—their moral and business reputations guarded from gossiping, destructive tongues.

And if Diane remained adamant and Anton Pellerin made no move in answer to Kurt's challenge, what, in the long term, did Kurt plan to do? Sooner or later, when he returned home to Neuchâtel, the truth about Diane must come out. Even before then he would have to admit it to what he believed to be Gesine's ignorance of it. Or was it her own duty, Nicola worried, to betray Diane to Kurt before she left the city herself? Yes, she thought. And yet——

Deliberately, bracing herself against reading into his kiss anything more than the passing curiosity he claimed, she refused to recall her instant of rapturous awareness that he meant to kiss her before he had done so. She hadn't resisted him . . . hadn't wanted to. She had known the danger of betraying her own need to him, and had courted it. But it hadn't got through to him, or else, as she half-suspected, he had known and had let her down lightly with his nonchalance about an 'isolated, uninvited kiss'. And now she wouldn't let herself think about it any more. *Must* not!

And did not—until some later phrase of Kurt's, only half heard or half understood, began to nag at her mind.

Something about her 'citadel' remaining untouched. No, unbreached—that had been the word which only now rang with some reference she ought to be able to recall; that was only just out of her memory's reach.

Long after she was alone that night, it continued to escape her. Until, when she had been asleep and had woken with a start, it seemed that her subconscious had found it. None too clearly, but clearly enough.

Rupert Brooke! The well-worn copy of his Collected Poems in the bookshelves of her room in her London hostel.

'. . . *a breach in the walls——*'

Yes, that was it. How did it go?

'*Love is a breach in the walls, a broken gate,*
*Where that comes in that shall not go again;*
*Love sells the proud heart's citadel to Fate——*'

What came next? No, she couldn't remember how it went on. But 'Love breaches the walls'. Ah, if only she could hope Kurt knew his Rupert Brooke and had been quoting! But of course he hadn't. It wasn't possible. Just the coincidence of a choice of words. As she lay back, self-pity and desolation flooding over her, she wished with all her heart that she hadn't ever read them herself. For Kurt hadn't even tried to pretend he was talking about love. Just curiosity, that was all.

The next morning, when he told her he had asked Gesine and Gregor Silber to join them and Hans for dinner that night, Nicola was momentarily too dismayed to demur. But later she rebelled.

Kurt wasn't being fair! Hadn't she *yet* convinced him he could trust her; or that she and Hans had never overstepped friendship? For one thing, opportunity was all and, as Hans claimed, they had had little enough of that.

Kurt must have known that Hans had been asking for the crumb of one more evening with her, and it had been bad enough when Kurt had blandly invited him to spend it at the villa, with himself as a kind of watchdog over them. But to make it yet another round table social affair, with Gesine's glamour dominating the scene, that was too much!

And there, her honesty had to admit, was partly the rub. Supposing Kurt had invited any other couple he could have named, she might have made the best of it and have suggested to Hans that, after dinner, they go out together. But to be forced to play hostess to Gesine, both of them aware of what each knew; she herself wary; Gesine revelling in the power she held—that, Nicola felt, would choke her. And on top of all, to hear in imagination Gesine's sly, double-edged comments if Hans and she did escape together for an hour—— No! This time, for the first time, she was going to fail Kurt socially. She would order dinner for three, not five. She and Hans would have the evening in each other's company, and she would take later whatever rap there was to come from Kurt.

She put her plans into action. She ordered the meal, told the Rallis she herself would not be in for it and telephoned Hans at his hotel. He was not in, so she left a message, asking him to ring her, and when he did so was rewarded by his eagerness to agree.

She asked him not to call for her and they made a rendezvous for a meal at a quiet restaurant on the lakefront. She planned to leave the villa before Kurt returned, and she wrote a note, telling him she would not be in for dinner.

It was a dreary day, heavy with humidity. Lowering clouds from over the mountains came in to meet others hanging over the lake. In the course of the morning the heavens opened to bring down torrents of rain over the city, to be followed by a 'dry' storm, with lightning knifing jaggedly down the sky, and thunder cracking almost instantaneously with it.

Nicola, lunching alone with small appetite for it, put down an odd malaise she felt to the electric atmosphere of the storm. During the afternoon her head began to ache and she felt less easy still. She would, at one time, have given anything not to have promised Hans. But when, at dusk, the sky cleared long enough to show the evening star winking out, she pulled herself together and went to meet him, though in the precautionary garb of mackintosh and rain-hood for her hair.

Though she was early, Hans was already waiting for her. For her aperitif she asked—unusually for her—for a cognac. The spirit put heart into her and she began to feel better. Hans, on greeting her, said, 'You realised I wanted to have you to myself for just this one evening? I am very grateful,' making her feel it had been worth the effort to please him, and worth whatever Kurt might have to say.

They had dinner, talking of everyday things as they ate, and afterwards, when Hans would have called a taxi to drive them somewhere, Nicola said on an impulse, 'Let's walk instead. I'd like the air.'

Hans looked dubious. 'Are you sure you want to? Supposing it rains again?'

'If it does, we can pick up a taxi then.'

'Very well.' Hans took her arm and by tacit consent they turned their backs on the lights and the speeding cars of the Bellerive Plage, walking instead towards the dark and quiet, at that time of night, of the commercial quays of Belgique and Ouchy.

They walked close to the edge of the quay, reading the names of the mixed craft moored alongside. Some were completely deserted. On others, whatever watch had been left on board seemed to be consoling itself with pop music from transistor radios. Lake water lapped and sucked at hulls; stays creaked; oil lamps swung and circled at mastheads, and as Hans and Nicola loitered or moved on, picking their way between the puddles in the uneven concrete, the storm clouds built high again and burst suddenly in renewed deluge.

They were wet before Hans had time to help Nicola to pull on her raincoat, and they were out of range of any cruising taxis. Hans looked about him, then offered a hand and said 'Come!' drawing her towards the narrow gangplank which led to the deck of one of the deserted boats. It was a small vessel, none too clean, and the deck was cluttered by piles of empty flower boxes. Both gangway and deck were slippery with wet, decaying leaves, but the overhang of an upper deck afforded some dry shelter and there Hans upended two wooden boxes and they sat down.

'This is trespass,' Nicola panted.

'Who is to know, and who could blame us?' But Hans managed to blame himself. 'I ought to have insisted on a taxi. If we wanted to walk, we could have asked it to wait or to pick us up. Now you are wet through.'

139

'We should still have got wet on a dash for the taxi,' Nicola pointed out. 'I'm no wetter than you, and I shall dry,' she claimed, though suppressing a shiver as she stripped off her coat and allowed Hans to hang it from a hook on the bulkhead behind them.

For a while they sat in silence, watching the vicious lash of the rain on the deck and the adjoining quay. Then Hans stirred and sat forward, both hands gripped between his knees. Not looking at Nicola, he said, 'I must say it's the last place I expected to choose for saying goodbye to you, Diane—a market boat in a thunderstorm! All the too few memories of you I've been saving up to take away with me—my imaginary you, at school at Vevey, and you, swimming with me and lying in the sun, and you, playing hostess at your brother's dinner table, and you, fabulously lovely at parties—and now, the one that will have to last me longest and that I thought I should treasure most—*this*!' And he sat back with a wry gesture of despair.

Not fully understanding him, for a moment or two Nicola did not reply. Then she ventured, 'But have we to say goodbye quite yet? You are staying for the Exhibition, aren't you?'

'Only for its first day. But this morning, when you offered me more time with you than I guessed I would have got, dining at your villa, I knew I must make this my real last time with you, in case you couldn't spare me another. And a "last time" I *had* to have—something to take away.' He hesitated, then turned and took her hand. 'You know I've fallen in love with you, don't you?' he pleaded.

She looked away. 'I—think so. I didn't want you to.'

'Neither did I, believe me!' His short laugh was embittered. 'But it happened, and I allowed it to, knowing there was no future in it, and now—well, now I have to pay. And lose you. And try to forget you. And—one of the worst things to be faced at the moment—I have to tell you why. That I must do— and tonight. So will you listen, Diane, please?'

Hearing him say in so many words that he loved her, she hadn't expected to escape the evasions and half-truths she must use to put him off, knowing that at their final parting she wouldn't be free to promise him even the continuing friendship he had the right to expect. But it seemed that she was to be spared this. *He* was renouncing *her*. Because, sensing that she didn't love him, he wasn't prepared to accept the second best of a friendship he thought she might offer instead? Or—the suspicion stabbed with almost a physical pain—had Kurt taken one telling step ahead of them both? Had he warned and convinced Hans already that a match between a mere Hans Durer and a Diane Thesige simply would not do?

Oh, he might, he *might* have trusted her to be gentle with Hans! The thought of how cruelly Kurt might have done her work for her made her turn impulsively to Hans.

'Don't tell me anything, if it's difficult,' she urged. 'You don't know what it means to me to hear you say you love me. But I'—she decided to use a truth she knew he would accept—'you see, I love someone myself who doesn't love me. So can't we agree to leave it there, without telling each other anything more? We've liked each other. For a little while we've been friends. Isn't that enough?'

He shook his head. 'For me, as I've told you, it has to be—well, not enough, but all I shall keep of you. But I still have to tell you why, loving you, I'm not asking you to marry me. So listen, please?' he begged again.

She didn't want to, dreading to hear just how ruthless Kurt might have been. But she let Hans begin and, listening, experienced a relief for which she hadn't dared hope. Kurt hadn't forestalled her after all! This was Hans's own dilemma that he had brought with him and that he would take back with him. This was dear, honourable Hans being his upright, loyal self. Putting her to shame with his total lack of self-pity. Simply stating 'This is so'; outlining his plans for a future he meant to control; scarcely even begging her understanding; merely asking that she listen.

For him, said Hans, there was, and always had been, a girl named Hilde. A distant cousin by marriage; a year or two younger than himself, but they had grown up together; boy-and-girl fond of each other, they and both their families had taken it for granted that they would marry each other 'one day'.

But before that day came Hilde had broken faith. She had engaged herself to another man who, when she had had a riding accident which at first had totally crippled her, had thrown her over.

She had partially recovered. Now she had only a spinal disability which reacted savagely to changes of temperature and to stress, with which she had had to come to terms in the faith that it would ease with time. But this, Hans claimed evenly, was a state of deferred hope that he could not ask her to endure alone. Besides, the frequently dank winters in Düsseldorf were

142

not good for her . . .

And so, before his trip to Lausanne, he had asked her to marry him. Some time after he returned he would be selling his share of the business on the Rosenstrasse to his brother-partner and after marrying Hilde, he planned to buy another, probably in Madeira or Grand Canary or Teneriffe, where the climate should do wonders for Hilde's health.

That was all, he said. Except that he hadn't wanted to fall in love with 'Diane', and had known all along that he must tell her the truth before he left. And except—and this was the only plea he made for her understanding—that he wanted to hope she knew there was a difference between 'in love' and 'loving'; that it was possible to experience both and still to choose the one he had pledged himself to before he ever came to Lausanne. More, he wasn't going merely to make a poor best of the lesser choice. He was going to make his marriage to Hilde *good*. So could he ask 'Diane' to wish him well in that? he appealed.

He must know he could, she told him warmly, adding, 'And I think I do understand that "in love" is a kind of infatuation that you can live down if you must, whereas "loving" is something you can make to last all your life.'

Hans's English was not equal to 'infatuation', but when she explained it more simply, he did not agree.

'No,' he claimed thoughtfully. ' "In love" is as sweet and real as "loving". It is more—dangerous, that's all. More easily hurt. More jealous. Less generous than loving. The perfection is to have both for one person and to get both in return, I think. But if one must choose for a lifetime, it is loving that wins, and

143

loving is something I have always felt for little Hilde. Yes, I know our marriage can march on it. It will make children for us, and we shall have each other and——'

He broke off there, stood abruptly and moved to the deckrail where he looked skyward, offering his hand, palm upward to it.

'It has stopped raining. Time to go,' he called back, and Nicola, pulling on her coat as she went to join him, knew she must respect his silence on all the things he had left unsaid.

They picked up a taxi on the Bellerive. To Nicola's relief the Silbers' hired car was not still outside the villa, but the lights all over the ground floor showed that Kurt was about, probably waiting to wither her with his criticism of her truancy.

Hans had asked the taxi to wait on the avenue and he came with her to the door. When she took her key from her bag his hand laid over hers stopped her from opening the door at once.

He said, 'Tonight we have talked all—and almost only—about me. But we have finished now. So far as you are concerned, I am—over. But just one question for you, Diane. This other man for you—would you say you are in love, or do you love, or both? Can you tell?'

She wished she knew for certain. 'Probably only in love,' she told Hans. 'I don't know him well enough to be sure of—the other, the lasting thing.'

Hans frowned. 'So? And he doesn't know you well enough either?'

(*When only curiosity is afoot . . .!*) 'Know me?' She heard her echo, unnaturally high, a little cracked.

144

'Know me? Why, he scarcely knows me at all!'

Then she wrested her hand free, managed a wintry smile for the concern she read in Hans's face and, using her key on the lock, went in to face Kurt.

# CHAPTER EIGHT

KURT, unsmiling, came to meet her in the hall. He watched as she threw her still damp raincoat on a chair.

'How did you get wet? Didn't Durer have a car?' he asked.

'To bring me home, yes. But after dinner we were walking, and we were caught in that last big storm.' She felt ill again, as if her head were too heavy to hold upright, and she could hear the thud of her heart. 'You got the note I left for you?'

'How otherwise could I know you had gone out with Durer?' he countered. 'But why did you cut across my invitation to him to dine here tonight?'

'Because I realised, that day in the Lausanne-Palace bar, that he was asking for just one evening with me, and when you told me you had asked the Silbers too, I knew he wouldn't get it. So I suggested to him we should go out together instead.'

'Leaving me to explain to my guests as to why you weren't here?'

'As it was only the Silbers who were coming, I thought you could.'

'Even though absenting yourself at such short notice was hardly within our terms of reference?'

Whatever was physically wrong with her stung her to sudden irritability. 'Don't you mean my terms of employment?' she retorted.

He shrugged. 'If we are being so blunt, yes!'

'Then I'm sorry.' Saying so almost choked her and as soon as the words were out she was denying them. 'No, I'm not,' she went on. 'It seemed the only thing I could do. I like Hans Durer and he likes me. He is good and sincere and—uncomplicated, and what he had to say to me tonight needed all the time and privacy that you wanted to grudge him, so I'm glad I gave him the chance. But now it's all said, and over, and finished. You don't have to worry any more that I shall take time out to see him again alone. I shan't— though at his will, not mine. And there won't be any after-problems from him either. He is honour bound to a girl in Düsseldorf, and when he leaves here he is going back to marry her and then taking her abroad. So you see? No Cinderella disappearing act called for from me; just Hans, taking himself off-scene by choice and for good! All very tidy, very neat, and I can only hope that you're s-s-satisfied——'

But the chattering of her teeth made a lame stutter of the final word of her defiant tirade. Dizzily reaching for a chair, she sat down, propping her elbows on her knees and making a shade of her linked fingers for her dry, aching eyes.

She was aware of Kurt's silent scrutiny. What he could be thinking, she felt too ill to care. After a moment he said, quoting her, 'Honour bound? Or love bound?'

She did not lift her head. 'Both. They've been sweethearts since they were children, and Hans asked her to marry him before he came to Lausanne.'

'Which doesn't seem to have cramped his style too severely with regard to you! I take it you knew nothing about this other girl until tonight? Yet he has pursued you ever since he arrived.'

'But there has been nothing serious between us. He has never——'

'Made love to you?'

'Never even kissed me—not even goodnight,' Nicola corrected wearily. 'For goodness' sake, what time or opportunity have we had for a love affair? And at least he was honest about this girl before he left.'

'Whom he was under no obligation even to mention to you if there'd been nothing between you,' Kurt commented shrewdly. 'But however that may be, I'd give a great deal to make him answerable for the state he's left you in tonight.'

She moved her head from side to side in weak dissent. 'I'm not *in* a state. Or if I am, it's not Hans Durer's fault. But if you won't understand about him and me, then I can't argue any more. I just want you to leave me alone. I——'

But though she summoned enough willpower to get to her feet, it failed her once she was there. She stood, fighting vertigo; heard through the roaring in her ears Kurt's incredulous echo—'Not in a state, indeed!' and then, after a lost moment of total oblivion, was aware of his arm about her, half guiding, half propelling her up the stairs and into her room.

She sank down on her dressing-stool and he stood over her.

'Well, whatever it is that has hit you, you've taken it badly,' he said. 'Tell me, what have you been doing this evening—apart from getting wet through and being politely discarded by Durer? I suppose he did find time, in the intervals of begging your sympathy,

148

to give you dinner? But what have you had to drink?'

'Only a glass of wine with dinner. Oh, and a cognac before it, because I was feeling rather odd, and had been all day.'

'And feeling ill, you still went out?'

'I didn't like to disappoint Hans, and I wanted to go.'

'Evidently. Well now, madam, you are going to bed and I'm calling a doctor to you.'

'Oh, not tonight,' she pleaded. 'Bed, yes—I'm only too willing, and I'll see a doctor if I'm not better in the morning. Meanwhile, perhaps Signora Ralli could bring me a hot water bottle and a hot drink or something, couldn't she?'

Kurt said, 'I'll bring them to you. I told the Rallis I would wait up for you, and sent them to bed. Do you have a sedative of any kind you could take with the drink to help you to sleep?'

'Only aspirins.'

'They'll have to do. Have them ready when I come back with the other things. And when I do, I expect to find you in bed. How long will you need?'

'Not very long.' She stood up, but was shy of making the smallest move towards undressing while he was there.

He waited. 'In *bed*,' he stressed. 'And if you're worried about being caught, daubed in night-cream and your hair in rollers, remember that sisters and wives share the privilege of being appreciated, even when they look their worst and know it. I'll give you ten minutes—no more.'

When he returned he brought two extra blankets which he dared her to throw off during the night. 'If it isn't merely an emotional thing, you've picked up some kind of germ and you must sweat the fever out.'

As she had said, she was past arguing that anything other than physical was the matter with her. He took her pulse and, in lieu of the clinical thermometer which the villa's equipment did not boast, he laid his hand first on her brow and then against each side of her throat, in an effort to test her temperature.

He stood back, studying her critically. 'On that evidence, I'd say you have a lot of fever to be rid of,' he said, and she agreed listlessly, 'I think I probably have.'

He waited while she drank her milk, and then a little longer.

'You think you may sleep now?' he asked at last.

'I hope so. Thank you——' she managed.

'Shall I leave your bedside light on?'

'No. My eyes can't bear it.'

'Then goodnight. And you—stay covered up, will you?' The last words were addressed to the bare arm she had flung out from under the blankets. He tucked it in again, brushed her cheek with a fingertip, then left her to the welcome darkness of the room.

It was after she had been alone for some time that her feverish mind latched on to a thought that was to become a kind of pulsing obsession for the rest of the night.

*Geneva!* She had to go to Geneva in a day or two's time. Had to be well enough . . . had to. However ill she felt, she must get up and dress and pack, and somehow get herself to Geneva . . . Geneva . . . Geneva. It became a thudding drumbeat, a devil's tattoo that went on and on and on.

Very early next morning Kurt was back, saying he had called a doctor and bringing with him Signora Ralli, clucking concern that she had not been summoned to Nicola overnight.

*Then* a timely bowl of her *zuppa alla cipolla*—the thick onion soup of her own native Piedmont—might have worked wonders. Or a good poultice of linseed for the chest. Or a cold compress for the head. But these sovereign cure-alls having been neglected, now —ah, who knew? she forecast darkly. To which Kurt's dry reply was that it was to be hoped the doctor might, as he left her to make Nicola as comfortable as possible.

An hour later the doctor had made his diagnosis—a virus infection that should answer to antibiotics. Nicola must stay in bed on the lightest of diets until a day or two after her temperature had dropped. Meanwhile, no stress; no worry. Her convalescence would probably be short. He would have some medication made up for her, and he would look in every day to ensure she was obeying orders.

'She can be well nursed?' he asked Signora Ralli at her bedside.

'Of course, *signor dottore*. I myself——'

'Good. Then a week or perhaps even less and we shall have you on your feet,' he promised Nicola, and left.

A week! Why, she couldn't afford to be ill enough to stay in bed even three days hence, let alone a week! When Kurt came to her after seeing the doctor out, she thrust up against her pillows, protesting feebly:

'He said I might be here for a week! But that's impossible. I've got to go to Geneva before——!'

'*Geneva?*' For a moment Kurt looked blank, then laughed shortly. 'My dear girl, you can forget Geneva. Geneva is out, as far as you are concerned.'

'But I must go. I can't stay here. You said——!'

'Never mind what I said before you contrived an alibi for yourself that will serve our purpose just as well.'

'An—alibi?'

His alight gesture indicated the room, her bed. 'Well, all this—what else? You won't be attending the Exhibition because you aren't well, which can be seen for the truth, and which is as good as a temporary flight to Geneva any day, don't you agree?'

She looked across at him, her aching limbs grateful for the reprieve from having to move from the cool of her bed, her worried mind taking in the argument and her whole spirit crying out against the cold-blooded, calculated reasoning of it that she had to accept as being all that a mere tool for Kurt's manipulation had the right to expect.

Her illness had incommoded his plans. No matter— he could readily adjust to others. Yes, for him it was as simple, and for her, as heart-tearing as that.

But he was kind. As was everyone else as soon as the news of her illness got round. Kurt had flowers sent in to her, and the fresh fruit she craved. He took his morning *café-complet* with her in her room and when she was able to listen, kept her posted on his final arrangements for the Exhibition. Other people called and rang up to enquire about her, and sent flowers and colognes and magazines. They all hoped she was going to be well in time to wish them Bon Voyage before they left Lausanne. Meanwhile she must know that she would be welcome whenever in the future she cared to look them up in the States or in Holland or in England or wherever. She had helped to 'make' their stay in Switzerland . . .

She was grateful that Kurt, with Signora Ralli acting as deputy dragon, discouraged visitors to her. If she were allowed to see any of the other ladies of the party, she could hardly refuse Gesine. Though whether or not Gesine had any wish to see *her* she did not know until, on the third evening after her attack, when she was feeling much better, Kurt played messenger for Gesine's excuses.

They came in the shape of a flask of exotic perfume and a note. Gesine had written:

'Really too bad for you, dear! A hideous anticlimax to a most successful campaign—so far. But I hope you will forgive me if I don't come actually looking for germs. They tend rather to make straight for me, and when I get back to Beirut after Kurt's show, I have a very full "little book" of dates I don't care to risk missing.

'Among them, London next month, when—by coincidence, of course, dear!—Kurt plans to be there too, though he tells me you won't be with him. Such a pity. But be very sure that I shall want to hear all about you, and who knows?—he may tell me that you have settled for marrying your correct and faithful young German. In other words, that you are changing your name . . .

'In the meanwhile, don't worry that you have left Kurt without a hostess for the Exhibition. I can guess he is hoping I shall offer to stand proxy for

153

young sister Diane, and such is the power of the man's charm, I may find myself doing just that. As ever——G.'

Kurt watched as Nicola tore up the note after reading it. He held out his hand for the pieces and dropped them into the wastepaper basket for her. 'I hope Gesine was properly tactful about her fear of catching the plague?' he queried.

'Yes, quite. She says she has a lot of engagements lined up, and she can't take the risk.' Nicola drew a long breath. 'She also says she is prepared to play your hostess for the Exhibition, if you ask her to.'

'I hadn't realised she needed asking. I'd rather assumed that she would.' Kurt paused to throw Nicola an oblique look. 'Would you be jealous if she did?'

'*Jealous?*' Her echo of the word, so cruelly attuned to her reaction, came out as a sharp rejection of the very idea. She repeated it more quietly. 'Jealous? Why should I be?'

'Good. So long as you are not. I only thought that, having filled the role yourself with such success——'

'Well, I'm not,' she lied gallantly. 'Like you, I expected she would. Although *I* thought you had said you couldn't ask a—a friend to act for you; that there were—reasons why you couldn't?'

He agreed coolly, 'Which there were, and are, though with regard to my obligation to Gesine, they don't obtain.'

(Because nobody is going to question the propriety of your inviting your future fiancée as your hostess?) Taking his answer to that for granted, Nicola did not ask it. She changed the subject instead.

154

'I suppose I shall be well in time to say goodbye to everyone before they go,' she said. 'They all seem to want to see me before they do.'

'Let's hope so. And I suppose you will be wanting to leave yourself soon after that?'

'Whenever you can free me. You'—she braced herself for the question—'you would tell me, wouldn't you, if you had heard anything about Diane in answer to your advertisement to Anton Pellerin?'

'Of course.' He looked surprised that she should ask.

'Then you haven't?'

'Not to date. But given a little more time, I haven't much doubt that I shall.'

Nicola shook her head. He knew already her opinion of that optimism. There was nothing to be gained by repeating it. And though for a moment she was tempted to tell what she knew, she caught back the impulse.

As he and Diane had each claimed at different times, she was torn between both their 'sides'. And though she meant to tell him the truth before she herself left Lausanne for good, she had to give Diane's bid for freedom and for love the very little time that remained between now and then. She owed Diane that.

Hans had sent flowers and he came to see her on the day before the Exhibition, when she was sufficiently better to sit up in her room.

'I feel so guilty about all this. It was my fault. I should never have allowed you to get wet that other evening,' he said.

'It wasn't that. Whatever I caught, I already had it

155

by then. I think I may have been running a bit of fever all day,' she told him.

'You didn't say so!'

'It was so slight then, I almost forgot about it.' Nicola added, 'Thank you so much for your roses. They were the first flowers anyone sent me.'

'I'm glad.'

They sat in silence after that, two people with a gulf of unspoken reserves between them. At last Hans said, 'I wanted to tell you—I'm catching the midnight plane for Düsseldorf tomorrow night and I shall need to leave the Exhibition for the airport by ten at latest. I think your brother said you won't be well enough to be there?'

Nicola shook her head. 'I'm afraid not. Doctor's orders.'

'Then we shan't be meeting again after this?'

'No. How soon do you plan to leave Düsseldorf again later?'

'I can't say. First I have to deal with the business that will have arisen out of my coming here. Then there will be all the machinery of handing over to my brother. Some weeks, perhaps; even a month or two.' Hans paused. 'I know, when we first met, I told you you should visit Düsseldorf, that I should like to show you round. But you won't come now, while I am still there, will you, Diane?'

She felt ashamed of the certainty with which she could assure him she would not.

She added, 'But believe, won't you, that I'm grateful for your telling me about Hilde, instead of just going away, as you might have done. And make her very happy, please, Hans—and be happy yourself?'

He stood up and set his chair tidily aside. 'Our marriage will take care of that, I think,' he said. 'Hilde and I know each other well enough to forgive and understand a lot. All our questions were asked and answered a long time ago. Which is important and good, and which I wish you were able to tell me about the man *you* love. It made my heart ache to hear you say he hardly knows you at all. Nor wants to? Nor ever will?'

'I doubt it.'

'But he is *in* your life? You see him often? You must go on doing so?'

'Not indefinitely.' Unable to bear any more of Hans's gentle probing, she attempted levity. 'It's all right. You don't have to worry about me, Hans. I shall —live.'

He agreed gravely, 'As we all shall. But if ever things change for you, think, won't you, that if I could know, I'd be very, very glad for you?'

'I'll remember,' she promised him, relieved that his 'If I could know' showed that he did not want to hear from her. As of course he never would . . .

After that they talked the everyday nothings of people saying their goodbyes. Hans hoped she would soon be quite better; she wished him Bon Voyage. But when he had gone Nicola realised that throughout the formal little exchange each had been telling the other, without the use of words, that this was the final parting of their ways; that, for their own different reasons, they would not seek news of each other again. The brief story of Hans Durer and 'Diane Thesige' was over.

157

That night Kurt was out to dinner. Nicola did not know where. The next morning the Exhibition opened at ten; Kurt had left the villa before eight and would probably not return until the small hours, after its midnight closing. Nicola, still confined to her room, neither expected nor had any visitors all day. But the Exhibition was an important feature of the local television news and at intervals she was able to watch scenes and interviews from it on the portable set which Kurt had hired for her use. After the general news bulletins at eight, when there was to be nothing more from the Palais de Beaulieu until ten, she listened to some music on the radio while she ate her supper from a tray and took a bath. She was sitting up in bed, idly watching the closing sequences of the previous programme, when the words 'News Flash' came on the screen, followed by the fading-out of both picture and sound.

On the blank screen they gave place to the wording:

Montreux. Staff And Guests Trapped In Serious Fire In Local *Pension*. Some Already Rescued, others Unaccounted For. Blaze Not Yet In Control

upon which the film was faded-in again for the duration of its last few minutes of running.

For a moment or two the flash had for Nicola only the small shock of a remote disaster—stark catastrophe for other people which had nothing to do with her. But almost before the announcer's voice came back, her mind's eye seemed to be reading the words again:

and knew by some strange prick of intuition that the
tall, narrow house on the Avenue Goncourt would
prove to be both the criminal and the victim of the
story the announcer had to tell.

Dispassionately he added details her sixth sense did
not need—'The Pension Areuse. An old house, of
narrow hallways and stairs creating "chimneys" for the
uprush of the fire——' and others which told not
nearly enough of all that she and all the other involved
listeners wanted to know.

The announcer apologised. Viewers would understand that the report was confused ... names of the
rescued and missing not reliably known at this stage
... Later bulletins would be issued as further news
came in ... And now over to the Thesige-sponsored
Horological Exhibition at the Palais de Beaulieu once
more——

For Nicola there followed a frozen moment of inability either to think or to do. Then thought returned
and upon thought, action.

Diane! Diane was there in that firetrap of a guest-
house, and no one of her own except Anton Pellerin
and Nicola knew it. Kurt didn't. Kurt could have seen
or heard both newsflash and news and still think it had
no bearing for him. But it had! *Kurt had to
know*——

Nicola was already out of bed, throwing off dressing-
jacket and nightgown and reaching for a minimum of
clothes before she rang for Signora Ralli.

When the woman came—'I find I must go to the

Palais myself,' Nicola said. 'Something very urgent I have to tell my brother. So ask your husband to call a taxi, please. It'll save time while I finish dressing.'

The housekeeper stared. 'You are going out, *signorina*? Into the night air? But the doctor said——! The *signore* too——! Could you not telephone him instead? Or send my Bertillo with a message for the *signore*?'

'No. I have to speak to him myself, and he might not be free to come to the telephone at once. I must go. So—a taxi, please, as soon as one can possibly get here.' While she was talking Nicola was thrusting into a sweater and pulling on slacks and tying a scarf over her hair. She snatched up a light coat, checked that she had money for the taxi and was downstairs almost on Signor Ralli's heels.

When the taxi arrived Bertillo Ralli went out to it with her.

'Signor Thesige will be returning with you, *signorina*? Shall Maria prepare a meal for him perhaps?'

'No. That is, I don't know when we shall be back. Don't expect us.' They were good people and Nicola felt guilty at the mystery she was making of her errand. But what else could she do?

The taxi sped, halted at red lights, raced between traffic jams; north through the city centre and out to the Palais de Beaulieu. From far off the sky was a crimson glow from the lights of the Palais; the lawns and flowerbeds of the great forecourts were floodlit and the car parks a'block with cars. Nicola asked her driver to park as close as possible to the main entrance, and they were lucky enough to find a slot from which another car had just pulled out.

'Wait, please. I shall be back.' She ducked from the cab, ran into the foyer, found a doorman whom she tipped liberally to go in search of Kurt who might be anywhere in any of the halls.

'We can have Monsieur Thesige paged, *madame*,' the man offered.

'No, I'd rather you found him privately, if you can.' She repeated the exact position of her taxi, returned to it herself and her tension mounting every minute, waited for Kurt to join her.

At last he was there, throwing open the door of the cab, peering inside.

'Nicola!' It was the first and only time in their association that he had failed to call her Diane. 'What on earth are you doing here? What do you want? What——?' His voice rasped with anger and bewilderment, both.

She sat forward, imprisoning his hand with her own on the edge of the cab window. 'I had to come. I'll explain. Please—it's urgent! It's—Diane. Your car, Kurt—is it handy? Will you take me to it?'

It seemed he had only heard Diane's name. 'Diane?' he echoed sharply. 'What about her? Has she —come back?'

'No . . . no. But I know where she is. And she is in danger, or could be.' Nicola was out of the cab by now. 'Kurt, *your car*! Where is it? You . . . we've got to go to Montreux. Tonight. Now, please——!'

She watched him frown. '*Montreux?* Diane——?'

'Yes.'

To her relief he took over from there. He paid off the taxi, threw one backward glance at the brilliance of the foyer and the rank upon rank of lighted windows, then strode away across the forecourt without another word.

Nicola matched his pace with difficulty. He scarcely acknowledged her presence until they were in his car and even then he had switched on and begun to edge out before he questioned, 'Montreux? How do you know? And where?'

The moment she had dreaded for so long! 'The Avenue Goncourt. A—a guest-house called the Pension Areuse. Did—did you hear a news-flash on television a little while ago—just before ten o'clock?'

Kurt shook his head. 'No. What?'

'A serious fire at this house. People trapped—no names, no details. But the fire still raging when——'

He cut into her hesitancy. 'No names? Then how? Why should you think *Diane* is involved, just from the news of this fire?'

'Because—I know she was there.' Nicola swallowed hard on the cold ache of her throat. 'Because I've known for some time now. I've been to see her there. She asked me to. She was alone—living-in as a reception-clerk. Anton Pellerin is in Montreux too, working for a garage. But they are not together, nor have been at all in—in the way you feared they were. They were just holding out on you. Diane said they meant to, indefinitely. But now——' Nicola's voice trailed away into silence.

Under Kurt's sure hand the car was almost clear of the heaviest of the city traffic, gaining the lakeside roads and speeding eastward to the open country. He stated levelly, 'You've known this. You've seen fit not to tell me. So you must have had your reasons. What were they?'

'I—meant to tell you before I left.'

'Indeed?'

'But, as Diane could convince me they had done nothing wrong, and were creating no scandal, I thought I owed it to her to have time to prove to you —well, all they wanted to prove. That they are really in love and have a right to their own lives. You see, I have met Anton Pellerin too, and I'm convinced he is sincere.'

'You met him when? And where?'

'He rang the villa one day when you were out. He had watched you leave. I met him by appointment at a café in the city. He didn't want to tell me where Diane was, but I made him. I told him it wasn't fair to you to keep their whereabouts secret, even if they weren't coming back.'

'Yet *you* withheld them from me!'

'I didn't mean to, until after I had seen Diane. I thought I could persuade her to get in touch with you herself, but *she* over-persuaded *me* that they had to hold out against you. They—they both trusted me, and I couldn't let them down.'

'And when and where did you see Diane?'

'I came over to Montreux while you had taken the party to your Neuchâtel works. I went to this Pension Areuse.'

'So when I told you of my advertisement to Pellerin, I suppose you felt you were arguing from strength that it hadn't a hope of being answered?' Kurt paused. 'Tell me, whose side *are* you on, and have been all along?'

She shrank from the cold acrimony she heard in his tone. But before she could reply he had drawn up at a roadside telephone kiosk.

'I'm going to make two calls,' he said. 'One to the Palais to say I've been unavoidably called away; the other to the Montreux Police—they may have more news by now. That should give you time to decide your answer to my question, and I shall want one, please.'

He got under way again before telling her that the news from Montreux was still confused and he had not waited for confirmation that the fire was now under control. He had thought it better to press on——

There followed a moment's silence; a waiting silence that she must break. She said slowly, 'You've every right to ask, I know. And I suppose the answer has to be "Both". But you've known that. You've accused me of being half on Diane's side before now. As she accused me of being on yours—— I've felt for her all the time I've been under my pledge to you. It hasn't been—easy. But at least I've done all you've asked of me as well as I've known how, and if this hadn't happened, I'd have gone on doing it until the—the end.'

Kurt agreed, 'Exactly. You've played to the letter the part I mapped out for you, and I can't fault you in it. But when I engaged you, I didn't buy either your emotions or your liberty to indulge in intrigue or your full loyalty? That is what you're saying, I take it?'

The sting of that was too cruel and she rounded on him. 'You've *had* my loyalty! As much, I think, as I've ever given to the service of anyone. And I haven't intrigued against you. I only delayed telling you something you would have had to hear in the end. I was

164

bidding for time for Diane, that was all. For the rest, you admit yourself, I have played my part, and I don't know what more you can want of me than that——!'

'No, you wouldn't.'

She hardly heard him as she plunged wildly on, 'And this I couldn't help or foresee. How could I? That I'd have to call you out from the Exhibition; force your hand before you were ready? All right! I know it's a crisis you might have been spared; the chance of scandal that you've managed to avert so far. There'll be questions asked ... the press will want to know, and Gesine Silber, having to make your excuses for you, will need placating too, won't she? Well, with Diane in the danger she might very well be, *I* thought I must risk all that. But perhaps *you* consider I should have coped alone? That I shouldn't have panicked and —and run for you? If I hadn't, would you have seen that as evidence of the loyalty you say you haven't had from me? Or as even yet more intrigue, I wonder?'

She was flinging wild, groundless charges and knew it; so many headlong words uttered only at the driving force of her pain. Sideways in her seat, she faced his set profile in silhouette and watched his jaw and lips harden as her voice died away.

'Have you finished?' he asked rhetorically. 'If so, may I make myself quite clear about one thing—or rather, two? The first—if you hadn't done just what you did tonight and had dared to act alone, I should have regarded that as a breach of faith that I couldn't forgive. And the second—whatever scandal or no that all this may spark off, it's of no account at all, set against Diane's safety or danger. Oh yes, and a third—— You can forget that snipe of yours about my need to "placate" Gesine. Because in fact, she wasn't affording me any support at the Palais this evening. She wasn't there.'

'Not *there*? But—— Why not?'

'Because she had decided to leave Lausanne on the afternoon flight for Beirut. Gregor Silber is following her tomorrow. If you saw anything that was shown on television, you must have realised the cameras wouldn't have missed her if she had been there?'

Nicola admitted, 'I did wonder. But when did she decide to go? In the note she wrote to me she said——'

'We dined together last night at her suggestion—without her cousin. She made her decision as a result.'

'And—you?'

'Gesine and I won't be seeing each other again.'

(What was to be read into that?) 'I thought you were to meet in London next month?' Nicola queried in bewilderment.

'If we do, it will only be in the way of business. On any other level—no. Our second parting is for good.' Kurt paused before his question. 'Why didn't you tell me Gesine had found out that you aren't Diane?'

Nicola drew a long, shuddering breath. 'You mean she told you last night that she knew?'

His slight nod answered. 'Also how she had learned it; that she had taxed you with it and that you had admitted it. Well, why?'

She couldn't tell him the truth! That, loving him, she had thought she couldn't bear to see him at Gesine's mercy, and so had gambled with the chance that, if their affair went as Gesine wanted, she might never need to use her power against him.

166

And so, as it was unthinkable to say, 'I loved you, and I tried to play for time for you, as I had for Diane,' she faltered instead, 'I—I suppose I thought the story would be safe with Gesine. Because anyway, if you were going to marry her, you would have to tell her the truth yourself after I went back to England and before she met your family.'

He pounced on the weakness of that. 'You aren't the best of liars,' he said dispassionately. 'What about this fellow who had recognised you? One careless or designing word from him could have set the whole thing alight. You must have realised that, surely?'

'I—well, I think I trusted Gesine not to let him know the news value of his having recognised me.'

'And finding Gesine as trustworthy as all this, didn't you wonder how it was I hadn't already confided the truth to her myself?'

'I thought perhaps you had decided that the fewer who knew it, the better.'

'And I don't believe you. You *must* have seen the danger—from this English journalist's nose for news, if not from Gesine, and possibly from both. And as one of them, I'm pretty sure, threatened you with exposure—which one was it?'

So much for trying to lie to him! In a low voice, Nicola said, 'There wasn't any danger from the Englishman, Mr Forsett. He didn't know enough. It was —Gesine.'

Kurt nodded. 'And she made the price of her silence—what?'

'Your proposal of marriage. She—she wanted to marry you very much and she meant me to know that she might use the story to smear all of us if she couldn't be sure of you very soon.'

'Exactly what she gave me to understand last night,' Kurt confirmed, then lifted both hands and thumped them back on the steering-wheel. 'But you——! You knew all this; knew the size of the threat; had known Diane's whereabouts even longer than that, and then you wonder that I question your loyalty. *Mon dieu*, I thought we were partners, yet you were ready to trust Gesine Silber when you wouldn't trust *me* with essentials I had a right to know! But no, that frigid detachment of yours had to show its independence of me, had to make its mark alone, had to——' He broke off to add with pseudo-patience touched with sarcasm, 'All the same, perhaps you'll search your memory now for anything else you may have held back?'

(Nothing but the truth which her pride couldn't bear to admit!) Nicola's silence ignored the taunt, and after a single swift glance her way, he didn't pursue the point. Until, a kilometre short of Montreux, he continued:

'Well, as a practical instance, whom are we looking for? Diane under an assumed name? Or her own?'

After the long break Nicola started at the sound of his voice.

'I—I didn't ask her,' she admitted. 'I don't know.'

'But you would have had to enquire for her at this *pension*?'

'No. She was at the recèption-desk in the hall, and we talked alone.'

'Pellerin's address then? Or this garage where he works?'

Nicola bit her lip. 'I don't know that either.'

'You don't? Well, well! Not such a perfect lonehand conspirator after all, it seems—missing out on a couple of simple facts we need and could use. There could be hope for us yet as a team!'

His tone was still caustic. But this time, meeting his glance, Nicola surprised a half-smile lifting the corners of his mouth and took some fleeting comfort from it.

He looked straight ahead again. 'But at least you know the way to this place and can direct me?'

'Oh yes.'

'Then get ready to do it. We're nearly there,' he said.

# CHAPTER NINE

THE Avenue Goncourt, which Nicola had last seen empty and sunbaked, was a mess of churned mud, deflated hoses and jostling, shouting crowds. By some freak of chance, the nameboard of the Pension Areuse had survived the fire, though now it leaned drunkenly against the front hedge of charred tamarisk. The building itself was a roofless shell with holes for windows, through which a couple of hoses were still trained to play on the ruins. It seemed clear there could be no one left inside, and this was confirmed by the harassed fire-officer whom Kurt approached.

The man thrust back his helmet and wearily wiped his face with a grimy hand. He was taciturn, making Nicola wonder how many times he had been taxed with the same questions.

'No. All out—nearly an hour ago,' he told Kurt.

'The staff, as well as the guests?'

'Staff or guests—how would I know, *mon vieux*? Just a bunch of frightened people to us,' he grunted.

Kurt placated him, 'I'm sorry. Ask a silly question—— But would you know where they were taken or went, after you got them out?'

The man shrugged. 'Our job was to get them out, which we did—those who had the sense to wait for us, that is. One or two didn't—at the price of some broken limbs, one hears.'

Kurt intercepted Nicola's horrified glance at the

upper floors of the blackened house and his steadying hand went to her arm and stayed there. He asked the officer:

'You mean some of them tried to jump? Then they at least could have been taken to hospital?'

'As most of them were, you'll find, though some may have been allowed to leave by now. But ask over there——' indicating a waiting ambulance. 'They will know better than I how many went.'

'Go back to the car and wait for me,' Kurt told Nicola. He pushed his way to the ambulance and rejoined her a few minutes later.

'They know no more than our friend. They are only standing by in case any of the firemen need attention. We'll try the hospital ourselves,' he said.

At the casualty ward of the hospital they met efficient but frustrating officialdom.

'The victims of the fire in the Avenue Goncourt? But yes, *monsieur*. Apply at the office, giving name or names, relationship and details. Then wait in the waiting-room for these to be checked,' Kurt was advised by the junior nurse he waylaid. But in the office the girl clerk had no trace of the admission of a Mademoiselle Thesige.

Kurt asked to be shown the list. When it was turned towards him he ran a finger down it; paused at a name and turned it back.

'Ah, my sister, under her professional name—Lois Mérand. We have been out of touch, and I hadn't realised that she might be using it. So as she has been admitted, may I see her, please?' he asked, his smile easy, bland and disarming.

The clerk seemed satisfied. 'Mademoiselle Mérand?

Your sister, *monsieur*? Yes, a second enquiry for her. The other—from her fiancé, I believe. But a few moments, *monsieur*, in the waiting-room. We have so many to deal with, you understand? Yes, yes, as soon as possible, of course——'

Outside the office Kurt glanced down at Nicola. 'You are wondering at my turn of clairvoyance, I daresay?' he asked.

'Not altogether. Lois, I've remembered, is Diane's second name.'

'As you say. And Mérand was our mother's family name. Combined, they were too much of a coincidence, and so I plunged. Rightly, it seems, as we aren't the first to enquire for her. In this waiting-room of theirs, we're probably going to find our friend Pellerin hoping to see her too.'

Kurt was right. Anton Pellerin was there, sitting forward at the end of a bench, his head dejectedly in his hands, staring at the floor. His were the last of all the eyes that turned anxiously at the sound of the opening door, but after a moment's hard stare at Kurt and Nicola he rose and came to meet them.

The two men measured each other in calculated silence. Then Kurt said enigmatically, 'So——!' and Nicola ventured to Anton:

'We had to come. Kurt had to know—— We heard about the fire on television and came over as soon as we could. Have—have you seen Diane? Or know any more about her than they have told us?'

Anton shook his head. 'Nothing since she has been in here. But I was there—at Areuse—when she was brought out. She was——'

He was interrupted by a middle-aged woman by

172

whose chair they stood. She sat forward to pluck at Kurt's sleeve.

'If you are talking about the young lady I saw Monsieur carrying to the ambulance, it was he who had brought her out himself. She was the first of two or three people he rescued before the firemen had their ladders erected. I was there, and I think you should know this, *monsieur*,' she stated, nodding.

'Thank you, *madame*.'

Kurt looked at Anton. 'Is this true?' he asked.

Anton shrugged. 'More or less. I was on my way to call for Diane, but the place was alight and the alarms had gone out by the time I turned into the Avenue. People were milling about; the fire engines hadn't arrived. It was just about nine o'clock; I knew Diane would have gone off duty at half past eight and would be in her room, getting ready to come out with me. She shared a room on the top floor with another girl on the staff, and the stairs made a kind of fire chimney, you understand?'

'But you went up?'

Another shrug. 'What else? Diane was alone there. The flames hadn't reached her room, but the smoke fumes had, and either in groping for the door or falling, she had knocked herself out and was only half-conscious when I brought her down. They took her from me at once—into the first ambulance. And I—went back to see what could be done for anyone else who might be trapped. Then the fire teams arrived and later I came here to wait for news, and am still waiting.' Anton paused. 'You know Diane has not been using her own name since she has been in Montreux?' he asked Kurt, who nodded.

173

'We didn't. But our mother's family name on the casualty list gave her away. And you, *monsieur*? By what name ought we to address you? It might be convenient to know.'

Anton's chin went up. 'By my own—why not? I'm only a baker's son and a motor mechanic. *I've* no high-class Thesige name to shield from scandal!' he snapped.

Kurt ignored the gibe. 'Good,' he said coolly. 'Then I wasn't wrong to address a personal advertisement to you in your own name? When you didn't answer it, I wondered.'

'And you actually thought I would answer it?' Anton demanded.

'If you saw it—and I did my best to ensure that you would—I expected you might.'

Anton's eyes blazed. 'Well, you were wrong, weren't you? Wrong then. Wrong now. Wrong about your own sister. Wrong about me. You claim to believe there's a price you could offer me for her and I'd take it? *Mon dieu*, Monsieur Kurt Thesige, what do you think I am? And if we were anywhere else than here, I'd——!'

His raised voice had brought every head turning their way, but the two men's hostility seemed oblivious of the curious eyes during the minute or two that ensued before the door opened again and a young nurse came in.

She checked a list in her hand. 'Monsieur Briand? Come, please—you may see your son. Madame Clairaux? And Monsieur Thesige—to see your sister, Mademoiselle Mérand——'

Kurt turned. 'Thank you. But we are a party, Nurse

—there are three of us.'

'*Three?* Oh——' The girl looked doubtful. 'I was told to call only one visitor at a time to each patient, *monsieur*.'

'Then two of us will wait. Monsieur Pellerin will go first.'

'Monsieur Pellerin?' She consulted her list. 'Ah yes, Mademoiselle Mérand's fiancé. Please come then, *monsieur*, will you?'

Anton did not move. 'You should go,' he growled at Kurt.

Kurt's brows went up. 'I? But it was you who saved Diane's life tonight, wasn't it?' he said.

'If I hadn't, someone else would have done, no doubt.'

'Nevertheless, you *did*. Besides, you'll be a more welcome visitor than I,' and turning a chair towards Nicola, Kurt sat down himself.

Anton grudged, 'Thank you. Shall I tell Diane you are here?'

'You will have to judge whether she is fit to hear it. She is going to have to know, isn't she?' Kurt returned.

When Anton had gone Nicola said, 'That was generous of you.'

Kurt shrugged. 'What else could I do? Between you, you have half persuaded me the man is in love with her, and until it's proved otherwise I'm prepared to give him the benefit of the other half of the doubt.'

'And will you tell Diane so when you see her?'

'Well, not quite so crudely, perhaps. And no, on second thoughts, I'll leave you to make my peace with her, while Pellerin and I repair to the nearest bar. I confess I don't take too kindly to the prospect of him as a brother-in-law, but both of us may mellow towards each other over a cognac or two, you never know.'

'You never know.' Nor, that night, did Kurt report what had passed between him and Anton while Nicola was with Diane, who, under sedation for shock, was already almost too drowsy to grasp the significance of Nicola's being there. Kurt, hearing that if all went well with her, Diane would be discharged the next day, booked a room for her in the same hotel as he installed Nicola in the small hours of the morning. That done, he was free to return himself to Lausanne for the final day and the closing of the Exhibition. After Diane's arrival at the hotel, she and Nicola would have a few hours together. But later in the day he wanted Nicola to travel back to Lausanne as, the following day, his guests for the convention would be booking out and they all wanted to take their leave of her.

Parting from him in the foyer of the hotel, 'If I get back to the villa in the early evening, will that do?' she asked.

'Oh yes. At a more civilised hour than this, I'll arrange for a hired car to come over for you. If you don't leave here until about six, Pellerin will be only too ready to take over from you with Diane, I daresay.' Then Kurt added the question he had asked once before. 'You are planning to leave Lausanne as soon as the others have gone?' but on the point of telling him, as she had done before, that she would go as soon as he agreed she could, a thought struck her.

176

'You are staying on, you said? Will the Rallis think it odd, my leaving the villa before you?' she queried.

'The *Rallis*?' Kurt's echo dismissed the quibble. 'My dear girl, in a couple of days' time from now, we may have brought the thing to the rubber-stamp conclusion we planned for it, but explaining your premature departure to the house staff is going to be the least of my problems after you've gone—the *very* least, believe me!' he said explosively, and went out to his car.

During the morning Diane was discharged from hospital and Anton brought her to the hotel during his lunch hour; he would be back to spend the evening with her before Nicola had to leave for Lausanne. It was from Diane that Nicola heard the outcome of what had passed between Kurt and Anton the evening before.

'According to Anton,' Diane reported, 'they are about as *sympathique* as oil and water, but at least Kurt listened, which was something. He tore Anton in shreds over the way we had gone about forcing his hand, and he dared Anton not to make me happy. But he said he wouldn't stand in the way of our engagement, and Anton says he seemed at least to have *heard* of people falling in love and marrying for it. Which wasn't at all the impression I had given him of Kurt, Anton says.'

'Hadn't they met in person before, then?' Nicola asked.

'Only at the garage where Anton worked at home. They were both so stiffnecked proud, I couldn't have brought them together if I had tried, and I doubt even

177

now if they will ever get on with each other.'

'Well, now they have met, they seem to have come to some kind of terms,' Nicola pointed out. 'And if, as you've said, you hardly know Kurt at all, had it occurred to you that—some time—he may have got badly hurt by love himself, and was adamant with you and Anton, in case you were heading for the same kind of pain?' (Though had that indeed been Kurt's motive? Or had it been his gesture of revenge for his own treatment by Gesine?)

Diane mused aloud, 'I wonder? I've never known—— But that wouldn't account for his sudden change of heart now.'

'He has met and talked to Anton now,' Nicola reminded her.

'Over a couple of drinks in a bar!' Diane scoffed. 'No, I'd rather think Kurt may have suddenly learnt for himself at first hand just what love is about. But you wouldn't know, would you, if you and he never got around to talking about personal things ... about yourselves? And yet you must know something about him if your guess is that he's been hurt by someone. How is that?'

Nicola told her then—all she knew about Gesine, doing her best to be fair, relating but not understanding what Kurt had told her of his second break-up with Gesine which he had claimed was final.

Diane queried, 'You don't know whose doing their parting was—Kurt's or hers?'

'No. They may have agreed to part. They may have quarrelled when she told him she knew the truth about me.'

'But she wouldn't have shown her hand to the point

of threatening him as you say she threatened you. He had to ask you about that. What did he say when you told him?'

Nicola did not need to think back. 'Nothing more about Gesine. Instead, he—rather turned on me for not trusting him with the things I'd known and had kept back.'

'And if he is still in love with her, I suppose he could forgive her in time. And yet how can he, knowing what he does about her? You don't think he will, do you?' Diane begged hopefully.

'I don't know. Perhaps that's what love is really "about", as you call it—accepting people for what they are, and forgiving even the worst in them.' With an effort Nicola shut away the picture of Gesine, conceding defeat for the moment, but still with enough nostalgic magic for Kurt for him to take her back. 'Anyway, what are your plans? When will you be going home?' she asked Diane.

'Kurt told Anton he wanted me to stay here until he leaves Lausanne himself. We'll go back together, and before Aunt Agathe returns from Paris. But I shall tell her what I did—to Kurt and to you—and everything. It isn't going to be easy. But I must—mustn't I?' Diane appealed.

'I'm sure you must. You would never be happy or at ease with her if you didn't. But there's no one else who will have to know, is there?' Nicola asked.

'Kurt promised Anton that no one should if he could help it.' As Nicola glanced at her watch, Diane hurried on, 'Oh dear, is it time for your car? So soon? And there's so much more to say! But you'll come back here before you go? Before I have to go home?

And you will come to Neuchâtel yourself later on? You must!'

Nicola shook her head. 'I can't see Kurt welcoming me there.'

'Why not, after all he owes you for what you've done for us? Besides, you would come at my invitation, not Kurt's.'

'To his house? I couldn't, Diane. He made it quite clear from the beginning that he was offering me a job; I accepted it, and when he has paid me for the time I've given to it, he'll owe me nothing and nor will you.' As Diane made to interrupt, Nicola forestalled her. 'Yes, I know, it's been a bizarre kind of job, with a lot of personal issues. But that makes it all the more necessary for it to finish after tomorrow, when the convention breaks up. As Kurt means it to finish, I know. He has already asked me twice how soon I plan to leave Lausanne after the other people have gone.'

'Getting rid of you! Well then, if you won't come back before I marry Anton, you'll have to come to us after I've left Neuchâtel. Anton hopes for a new job in Zürich, so you will come there instead? You will promise, Nicola, *please*?'

Zürich instead of Neuchâtel ... Lausanne ... Montreux! As if every frontier of Kurt's country wouldn't be closed to her in the foreseeable future, thought Nicola. But unable to tell Diane so, she promised, 'Perhaps,' and Diane was reluctantly content with that.

Anton had joined them before Nicola left for Lausanne. Arms entwined, close ... sure of each other, they saw her off from the steps of the hotel.

'*Au 'voir!*' they called, waving, as the car drew

away.

'*Au 'voir!*' Nicola waved back, her smile a mask and her eyes a mist of unshed tears she was thankful they could not see.

Kurt was not at home when she arrived. She heard him come in while she was doing some preliminary sorting of her things, preparatory to packing. He was ready with an aperitif for her when she went downstairs and they dined opposite to each other at the round dining-table.

He asked after Diane, saying he planned to go over to Montreux again after he and Nicola had taken leave of his guests the next day. Would Nicola care to go with him?

She thanked him but refused. 'I've said goodbye to Diane, and I'll write. No, I'll stay and do my packing and book my flight out,' she said.

'Your flight? I'll see to that for you.' Kurt went on to describe the Exhibition's second day which, like the first, had been an outstanding success, resulting in excellent business for everyone. They went on to talk about general things and adjourned to the salon for their coffee.

Nicola was ill at ease, desperately aware that she should be registering for her memory every look or trivial word they exchanged during an evening which was likely to be the last she would spend with him. Instead she was tensed for the embarrassment she could not escape—that of hearing him ask her what he owed her for her services and insisting that she name a figure, as she knew he would.

At every small silence that dropped between them

181

she waited for the question. But before it came she suddenly remembered something she had forgotten to do.

'Diane's driving licence!' she exclaimed aloud. 'I meant to return it to her. Would you take it instead?' she asked Kurt.

'Yes. Let me have it before I go over tomorrow.'

'You can have it now. It's in my bag.' After pouring coffee for them both she had moved over to the window seat to drink her own, leaving her bag on the coffee table. Kurt had sipped his, pacing the room, and after returning his cup to the tray, he had continued a restless prowling which had brought him back to the table as Nicola half rose to go for her bag.

He touched it. 'In here?'

'Yes.'

'Don't move. I'll bring it.'

She had left it open. Kurt took it up by its corner; between them they fumbled its handing over and most of its contents showered out at Nicola's feet.

'I'm sorry——'

'It was my fault——' Kurt, on his knees, was gathering feminine jetsam; Nicola picked out the small individual wallet which held Diane's licence and handed it to him—to remember too late that, behind the other of the wallet's talc windows, she had tucked the flashlight snapshot of Kurt at the Evian Casino. She made to take the wallet back; he held on; she watched him open it idly—and stare, first at the snapshot and then, still kneeling, up at her.

'This wasn't here when I gave you the licence to carry.' He glanced again at the background to his figure. 'It hadn't been taken then. It was done at

182

Evian, surely? Right?'

Nicola felt colour flood her face and throat. 'Yes. I bought it from the man who was selling them.'

There was a curious, choked quality to Kurt's short laugh. 'You paid good francs for a photograph of me! My dear girl, why?'

She cringed from his astonishment. 'He was selling them,' she repeated lamely.

'But you didn't have to buy! Nor keep it in the modern version of a locket. Why?'

'I thought it was gòod of you. And'—she met his eyes in despairing defiance—'I—wanted it. *And* wanted to keep it.'

There was a long pause. Then the little wallet joined the rest of the clutter on the floor; Kurt's hands went over hers in her lap and, dropping his head on the clasped mound, he muttered, 'My dear, my dear! And I didn't know——'

She sat upright, very still. Kind! He was being *kind*—too kind to face the naked avowal of love her look and words had made him, he was pitying her, cushioning her pride, beginning to tell her that if he had guessed at her plight, he would have warned her that there was no future to loving him; that he had been blind to what had happened to her, and was sorry, and that was all.

But now——! Now he had lifted his head, was standing, drawing her to stand too, his hands spreading on each side of her face, his mouth finding hers in a kiss to which her own lips responded in rapture ... giving ... and taking; snatching at the miracle while it lasted. As it could not. Because this was Kurt taking pity for her too far. Didn't he know what it was doing to her? Didn't he *care*?

At last his hands went to take hers. Holding her back from him, he studied her face as if he were learning it, feature by feature.

'And to think,' he said slowly, 'that all I had dared to plan for this evening was to ask you if you would see me when I go over to London next month!'

'All—all you had *planned*?' Nicola's echo was blank.

'Planned! I've had to rehearse for hours what you might say if I asked you; how tactfully you would say No. And then—chance gives me this blessed bonus—that apparently you bear me so little grudge that you want a memento of me. I don't know what that says. I hardly dare ask. But at least, my love, my *love*, it allows me the short cut of daring to ask in the only way I know—— This!' And his arms went wide in invitation before they closed about her and his searching lips were demanding the surrender her body and spirit were only too hungry to give.

For a while there was only sensation—a warm, spreading pleasure in each other that blocked even thought. Then, aware again—— Why, this isn't pity, nor kindness, nor a sop for my pride. It's love! Kurt, wanting me, as I want him! Nicola was thinking as he held her away again to stare at her in a kind of incredulous wonder.

'Well, *ma mie*, do we mean the same thing—at last?'

She moistened lips that still felt shaped to his kisses. 'I—suppose so,' she said. 'But I didn't know. I thought you——'

'Even though I tried to tell you before—by the

184

same primitive means? On the ramparts at Sion—do you remember?'

'I thought you had guessed how badly I needed you, and you were being kind to me; saving my face.'

'Kind! I was in an agony of wanting you, and when you brushed me off, I confess I needed to hurt you. So! I thought. I'm just another of the men she claims to have taken in her stride and put out of mind. That was why I agreed it had had no more meaning for me than for you——'

'And left me to puzzle half the night as to whether you had known you were quoting an English poet on Love when you said my "citadel" was still unbreached!' Nicola teased shyly.

Kurt's eyes narrowed for the smile she had come to delight in. 'I once labelled you *La Belle Dame Sans Merci*, didn't I? So if I know my Keats, why not also my Rupert Brooke? Don't your schools study our French romantic poets in return?' he teased back.

Nicola's laugh was a sound of pure happiness. 'Then you did know? You *were* talking about love? But you called it mere—curiosity. And said you had experimented in the same way with Gesine.'

'And had proved what I hoped—that she had nothing for me any more. Nor I for her in the old way; only, now, as a social and financial scalp. Now, I imagine, as widowhood doesn't carry enough prestige for her, she may settle instead for cousin Gregor's money and doglike devotion. But, my darling, I'm a man! I had loved Gesine, so naturally I was intrigued by the possibilities she offered when she reappeared in my life.'

'But supposing she hadn't come back? One day,

would you have gone to find her?' Nicola asked.

Kurt flicked her chin with a forefinger. 'You *are* jealous! That's a good sign. No. She had hurt me without cause; she had chosen not to wait until I could offer her more than prospects, and wounded pride is a great spine-stiffener. No, I would never have sought her out. And you shouldn't belittle curiosity, *mignonne*. Don't you know that every love affair in the world begins with it—with all the questions of how and when and why just this one precious person should have happened to you; all the hankerings-to-know that you can't get answered soon enough? As I crave to learn everything about you. You too, about me?'

'Everything, Kurt. So much.' Her tone was heart-felt.

'And Durer? What about him?'

'He had been frank with me, and before he left I told him I loved someone I realised didn't know me at all. Not enough to trust me, anyway.'

'As you, madam,' Kurt retorted, 'weren't prepared to trust me! And besides Durer, any one of the men you were meeting could have been taking you from me while I was forced to keep you at arm's length for the sake of our plot. Trust you entirely? Well, knowing now what I've felt for you, do you imagine I could?'

Nicola chided gently, 'You can't have it both ways, Kurt. I couldn't be the frigid siren you've made me out, *and* a willing prey to any man who threw me a glance. And who did—except Hans, in passing?'

Kurt claimed, 'I, for one. And when you walked out on me to join Durer that night and came back, ill and

distraught, after being with him, I could have——!
And what about Gesine's parting shot—that I ought
to ask you about the man you have met clandestinely
at bars in the city? Who is he? If Gesine wasn't
merely being Gesine at her most malicious, have I got
to be jealous of him too?'

'Someone I've been meeting? Oh——!' As light
dawned, Nicola threw back her head and laughed.
'That was Diane's Anton! Gesine saw us together and
made a great virtue of not telling you that your little
sister had a boy-friend. I met Anton just that once at a
bar on the Rue Liseron. I told you——'

'So you did. But you see, don't you, what my
jealousy fed on? So little, and poisoned by stark fear
into so much.'

'Yet you said just now that it was a good sign I
could be jealous,' Nicola accused.

'Ah, "could be" is one thing. "With cause" is
another. There was no cause for you to be jealous of
Gesine's acting as my hostess for the Exhibition. But I
wanted to prod you into admitting you were.'

'Well, I admit it now. Besides, when you said there
was no longer any reason why you shouldn't invite
Gesine, I thought you meant that nobody would question your asking your future fiancée.'

'Whereas, in fact, there were two quite different
reasons. The first—that everyone knew you were ill.
And the second—that I could call on Gesine, adequately escorted by Gregor Silber and occupying a
luxury suite at the Beau Rivage, without an eyebrow
being raised. By no means the same problem as I had
at the outset—of needing to instal a "Diane" under
the same roof as myself, with only a cook and a house-

man for chaperons. Do you see?'

'Mm——' Pretending reluctance, Nicola added, 'At the time, though, I don't believe you cared whether I "saw" or not.'

Kurt chuckled wickedly. 'As I said, a little healthy doubt does no real harm. All the same, don't'—taking her back into his arms, he punctuated each word with a kiss—'don't . . . try . . . mine . . . too . . . far!'

For a while they teased on, skirmishing with words in the wary advance-and-retreat of lovers not yet quite sure of each other, nor of the wonder of its all having happened for them. The questions! *When did you know? What made you hope? Did I ever——? Supposing we hadn't——? Supposing—supposing——?* All asked and pondered and answered as eagerly and newly as if they weren't common to every two people in love and in search of each other the whole world over. And for Nicola, one question she had for Kurt, a little afraid of his answer.

She ventured it at last. 'Kurt, something I haven't understood. After suffering so much over Gesine's rejection of you because you had no prospects, why were you as bitter as you were about Diane and Anton for much the same reason?'

He did not answer at once. Then—'Do you feel you can't forgive the truth, if it has to be that I was only hitting back blindly at Gesine through Diane?' he queried.

Nicola lifted frank eyes to his. 'I haven't prejudged it. If that is the truth, I can forgive it. And understand it. It was just that I had to know.'

Kurt said very slowly, 'And how I wish I knew for certain! Of course I had to convince myself that I was protecting Diane in good faith. But was I? And by the time I had fallen in love with you and was cured of Gesine, Diane had escaped me, and it would be hard to prove my motives either way. So there it is, my heart—I just don't know.'

Nicola said gently, 'I believe I'm more grateful that you admit to the doubt than if you had claimed to be sure. Anyway, Diane is content with the way things are. And perhaps she was nearer the mark than she knew when she asked me today if I thought you could have fallen in love yourself.'

'To which you said——?'

'I didn't encourage the idea. But now—Kurt! Having to tell her now that you have, and that—for you— it's me! She will think I was deliberately stalling! What *will* she say?'

'*Chut!* Leave it to me. Tomorrow, after we have shot our last flights of this campaign, I shall carry you over to Montreux, wheel you in and—"*Alors, Diane! En voici ta belle-soeur future,*" I shall announce, and she had better be thrilled with the prospect,' Kurt threatened darkly.

Nicola sighed happily. 'How you dismiss hurdles in your path, almost as if they weren't there, don't you, Kurt? However, Diane said once she wished I were her sister. So let's hope she will settle for me as a sister-in-law instead. But what about the problems you accused me of leaving with you when I went back to England? What were they?'

'Hurdles that aren't there,' he retorted promptly. 'And the worst of them then—learning to forget you, if I must. But now—now we've sworn our fealty for good, now I needn't—need I, my young squire?'

Nicola dimpled demurely, taking her cue. 'I—hope not, my liege lord!' she said.

But her true answer was in the straining of her arms, holding him close, in the pounding of her heart near to his, and in the passionate promise of her kiss.

**To our devoted Harlequin Readers:**
**Fill in handy coupon below and send off this page.**

# Harlequin Romances

## TITLES STILL IN PRINT

- ☐ 51009 NURSE AT FAIRCHILDS, M. Norrell
- ☐ 51010 DOCTOR OF RESEARCH, E. Houghton
- ☐ 51011 THE TURQUOISE SEA, H. Wilde
- ☐ 51012 NO OTHER HAVEN, K. Blair
- ☐ 51013 MARY INTO MAIR, J. Ray
- ☐ 51014 HOUSE OF LORRAINE, R. Lindsay
- ☐ 51015 SWEET ARE THE WAYS, E. Summers
- ☐ 51016 TWO PATHS, J. Macleod
- ☐ 51017 ATTACHED TO DOCTOR MARCHMONT, J. Shore
- ☐ 51018 HOSPITAL IN THE TROPICS, G. Fullbrook
- ☐ 51019 FLOWER OF THE MORNING, C. Conway
- ☐ 51020 NO JUST CAUSE, S. Barrie
- ☐ 51021 FOLLY TO BE WISE, S. Seale
- ☐ 51022 YOUNG ELLIS, M. Hilton
- ☐ 51023 THE SWEET SURRENDER, R. Burghley
- ☐ 51024 THE HOUSE OF DISCONTENT, E. Wyndham
- ☐ 51925 SURGERY IN THE HILLS, I. Ferrari
- ☐ 51026 DOCTOR IN CORSICA, E. Gilzean
- ☐ 51027 THE LONELY SHORE, A. Weale
- ☐ 51028 THE MASTER OF NORMANHURST, M. Malcolm
- ☐ 51029 CHOOSE WHICH YOU WILL, M. Burchell
- ☐ 51030 THE BLACK BENEDICTS, A. Charles
- ☐ 51031 FLOWERING DESERT, E. Hoy
- ☐ 51032 BELOVED TYRANT, V. Winspear

~~~~~~~~~~~~~~~~~~~~~~~~~~~~

Harlequin Books, Dept. Z

Simon & Schuster, Inc., 11 West 39th St.
New York, N.Y. 10018

☐ Please send me information about Harlequin Romance Subscribers Club.

Send me titles checked above. I enclose .50 per copy plus .15 per book for postage and handling.

Name ....................................................

Address ...............................................

City ................ State ............ Zip ...........